Kate Hoffmann's Mighty Quinns are back—and this time, they're going Down Under!

All Quinn males, past and present, know the legend of the first Mighty Quinn. And they've all been warned about the family curse—that the only thing capable of bringing down a Quinn is a woman.

These sexy Aussie brothers are about to learn that they can't escape their family legacy, no matter where they live. And they're about to enjoy every satisfying minute of it!

Watch for:

THE MIGHTY QUINNS: BRODY
June 2009

THE MIGHTY QUINNS: TEAGUE
July 2009

THE MIGHTY QUINNS: CALLUM
August 2009

D0562021

Dear Reader,

Whenever I begin a new set of Quinn books, it seems like a daunting task. I worry about whether I'll be able to find heroes who live up to the rather formidable reputation built by the Quinns who came before them! But once I get into the stories, I realize that when it comes to the Quinns, every one of them lives up to that reputation—and more.

Callum is the last of the QUINNS DOWN UNDER and number fifteen in the series. It all began with a police detective in Boston named Conor. I never thought I'd be traveling the world looking for new branches of his family.

Will there be more Quinns in the future? Probably. Because we all know it's hard to keep a good man— or a family of them—down!

Happy reading,

Kate Hoffmann

Kate Hoffmann

THE MIGHTY QUINNS: CALLUM

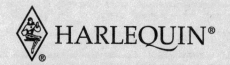

TORONTO • NEW YORK • LONDON
AMSTERDAM • PARIS • SYDNEY • HAMBURG
STOCKHOLM • ATHENS • TOKYO • MILAN • MADRID
PRAGUE • WARSAW • BUDAPEST • AUCKLAND

Recycling programs
for this product may
not exist in your area.

ISBN-13: 978-0-373-79492-8

THE MIGHTY QUINNS: CALLUM

www.eHarlequin.com

Printed in U.S.A.

ABOUT THE AUTHOR

Kate Hoffmann has been writing for Harlequin Books for fifteen years and has published nearly sixty books, including Harlequin Temptation novels, Harlequin Blaze books, novellas and even the occasional historical. When she isn't writing, she is involved in various musical and theatrical activities in her small Wisconsin community. She enjoys sleeping late, drinking coffee and eating bonbons. She lives with her two cats, Tally and Chloe, and her computer, which shall remain nameless.

Books by Kate Hoffmann

HARLEQUIN BLAZE
340—DOING IRELAND!
356—FOR LUST OR MONEY
379—YOUR BED OR MINE?
406—INCOGNITO
438—WHO NEEDS MISTLETOE?
476—THE MIGHTY QUINNS:
        BRODY
482—THE MIGHTY QUINNS:
        TEAGUE

**HARLEQUIN
SINGLE TITLES**
(The Quinns)
REUNITED
THE PROMISE
THE LEGACY

**HARLEQUIN
TEMPTATION**
 933—THE MIGHTY QUINNS:
        LIAM
 937—THE MIGHTY QUINNS:
        BRIAN
 941—THE MIGHTY QUINNS:
        SEAN
 963—LEGALLY MINE
 988—HOT & BOTHERED
1017—WARM & WILLING

To my readers in that wonderful land down under.

Prologue

Queensland, Australia—January 1997

"YOU KISSED HER?" CAL QUINN stared at his younger brother Teague in disbelief. It was one thing to kiss just any girl, but quite another to kiss a Fraser. Harry Fraser and Cal's dad were in the midst of a land feud, a fight that had gone on for years.

"I'm not spilling my guts to you boofheads," Teague said. "You'll tell Dad and then he'll lock me in my room until it's time for me to go to university."

Cal turned his gaze to the horizon. He and his brothers had spent the day riding the fence line along the west boundary of Kerry Creek Station, looking for breaks. On their way back to the homestead, they'd decided to make a stop at the big rock, a landmark on the station and a favorite spot for him and his brothers. They'd discarded their shirts in the heat, their bodies already brown from the summer sun, and crawled up on top of the rock.

"Dad would be mad as a cut snake if he knew what you were doing," Cal warned. "He hates Harry Fraser. All the Frasers."

"There are only two. Hayley and her grandfather. And Hayley doesn't care about the land."

Cal scowled. "Still, you shouldn't be talking to her. It's—it's disloyal."

"Oh, nick off," Teague muttered, growing impatient with the conversation. "You can't tell me what I'm allowed to do. You're not the boss cocky on this station."

Cal's temper flared. The hell he couldn't. He was the oldest of the three Quinn brothers and if Teague or Brody were doing something that might hurt the family, then it was Cal's duty to step in. "I will be someday. And when I am, you won't be kissing Hayley Fraser."

"If you tell Dad about—"

"I kissed a girl," Brody confessed. "Twice."

Cal leaned forward to glare at his youngest brother. Brody had always done his best to keep up, but he usually didn't resort to lies. "Twice?"

"Yeah," Brody said. "Once with tongue. It was kind of nasty, but she said we should try it. I thought I'd give it a fair go."

Brody had been living in Sydney with their mum, attending a regular school filled with real girls. He'd been to a proper dance and played footy with his school team and went to the flicks almost every weekend. Maybe he was telling the truth. If he was, then at fourteen, Brody had already passed Cal in worldly experience.

"Tongue?" Teague asked. "What does that mean?"

"When you kiss her, you open your mouth and touch tongues," Brody explained. "It's called French kissing. I guess the French do it all the time."

Teague considered the notion, his eyebrow raised in suspicion. "So who opens their mouth first, the guy or the girl?"

"Whoever wants to French kiss," Brody said. "If you don't want to do it, you just don't open your mouth. It's probably not so good to do if you're sick. Or if you have food in your mouth. Or if you haven't brushed your teeth."

Cal listened as his brothers discussed their experiences with girls, unable to add anything to the conversation. Cal was seventeen, yet he'd never kissed a girl, or touched a girl, or even carried on a conversation with one his own age. He'd lived on the station his entire life, miles from any female worth talking about.

Sure, he'd been to Brisbane a bunch of times with his family and he'd seen lots of pretty girls there. And his cousins had visited Kerry Creek when he was younger, and some of them were girls. But he'd never gotten close enough to…

He knew what went on between men and women. He listened to the jackaroos after they'd come back from a weekend in town. And he'd discovered self-gratification and teenage fantasies years ago. But he wanted to know about the real thing. Sex. Something that Teague and Brody might end up experiencing long before he did.

Cal had considered going into Bilbarra the next time the jackaroos took a weekend off and find himself a willing girl. He was old enough. His mother might disapprove, but she was living in Sydney and would have no idea what he was up to.

As for his father, Jack Quinn had left his two eldest sons to their own devices since the separation. Brody was out of his control in Sydney, but Teague and Cal had only Mary, the housekeeper, to watch over them. Though she was strict about schoolwork, and their father firm about station chores, Cal and Teague were allowed to spend their free time in whatever way they chose.

"Mac and Smithy said they'd take me into town the next time they went," Cal said, trying to maintain an air of cool. "They know a lot of women in Bilbarra."

"Yeah, only they all live at the knock shop," Teague said.

"Not all of them," Cal said. Though the boys did frequent the local brothel, they also spent time at the pubs. From what the jackaroos had told him, the brothel in Bilbarra was still a well-kept secret, one almost everyone in the territory knew. But there were other places in Oz where that type of thing was perfectly legal.

Maybe that's what he needed to do. Go find a place like that, pay his money and have done with it. He'd ask for a pretty girl, one with long hair and a nice body. And he wouldn't need to be embarrassed by his lack of experience. He'd be paying for a tutor.

Something would have to change. Cal had always dreamed about running Kerry Creek someday. But if he never left the station, there wasn't much chance of meeting females. Maybe he ought to do like Teague and make plans to attend university for a few years. He could study business, learn things that would make him a better station manager and at the same time, find a wife.

But the idea didn't appeal to him at all. He felt comfortable where he was. He'd learned how to run the station from watching his father. And he loved the work, loved the animals and the people who populated Kerry Creek. There was nothing more beautiful to him than a sunrise over the outback and nothing more peaceful than the sounds of life all around him at day's end.

Cal lay back on the rock and stared up at the sky, linking his hands behind his head. Though he wanted to believe the opposite sex might find him interesting, Cal knew life on an outback cattle station wasn't all sunshine and roses. His mother had left Kerry Creek just six months ago, unable to stand the isolation any longer.

Still, there had to be girls who liked riding horses and mustering cattle and fixing fences. Girls like Hayley Fraser. It might take a while to find someone like that, but when he did, maybe he could convince her to visit him on Kerry Creek. If she liked it, he would ask her to stay.

"I've seen lots of knockers, too," Brody said.

"Yeah, right," Teague said. "In your dreams, maybe."

"No, I'm not lying," Brody said. "Me and my mates go down to Bondi Beach on the weekends and there are girls sunbaking without their tops all over the place. You just walk down the beach and look all you want. You don't even have to pay."

Cal cursed softly, then sat up. "Is that all you droobs can talk about? Girls? Who needs them? They're all just a big pain in the arse anyway. If you two want to sit around sipping tea and knitting socks with the ladies for the rest of your life, then keep it up. I've got better things to do with my time."

He slid off the rock, dropping to the ground with a soft thud. Cal grabbed his gloves from his back pocket and put them on, then swung up into the saddle, shoving his hat down on his head. "Well, are you two coming? Or do you need help getting down?"

Teague and Brody glanced at each other, then slid to the ground, their boots causing a small cloud of dust to rise. "Come on, I'll race you back," Cal challenged.

"I'm in," Teague said, hopping on his horse and weaving the reins through his fingers.

"Not fair," Brody complained. "I haven't ridden in four months."

"Then you better hang on," Cal said. He gave his horse a sharp kick and the gelding bolted forward. The sudden start surprised his brothers. They were just getting settled in the saddle while he was already fifty meters in front.

This was what he loved, the feeling of freedom he had, the wind whistling by his ears, the horse's hooves pounding on the hard earth. He was part of this land and it was part of him. And if staying on Kerry Creek meant giving up on women altogether, then he'd made the choice already. This was home and he'd spend his life here.

1

May 31, 2009

THE SUN WAS BARELY ABOVE the horizon as Cal got dressed. He raked his hands through his damp hair, the thick strands still dripping with water. He usually showered at the end of a long workday rather than first thing in the morning, but he'd come in so late last night that he'd flopped onto the bed and fallen asleep with his dusty clothes on.

Strange how a year had flown by so quickly. It seemed like just last month that they'd finished the mustering and now they were about to start all over again. He should have been accustomed to the rhythms of the station by now, but the older he got, the more Cal was reminded that time was slipping through his fingers.

He sat down on the edge of the bed and pulled his boots on, then rolled up the sleeves of his work shirt. As he reached for his watch on the nightstand, Cal noticed the letter he'd received from the matchmaking service sitting out. He grabbed it and shoved it into the drawer. Better not to let anyone know what he was contemplating, especially Mary, the station housekeeper. He'd be facing the Aussie inquisition over the dinner table if she found out.

He'd discovered the Web site a few months back—OutbackMates—an organization devoted to finding spouses for country men and women. He'd filled out the application last week and sent it in with an old photograph of himself. According to the letter, his profile would appear on the site next week. It was a bold move, but he was nearing thirty and he hadn't had a long-term relationship with a woman for…ever.

The station kept him so busy that he rarely took more than a day or two away. Cal knew all the single women in Bilbarra and not one of them would make a suitable wife. The past few years he'd been forced to go as far as Brisbane for feminine companionship. Unfortunately, the single women he'd met there weren't interested in romance with a rancher who lived five hours away, either—except when he happened to be in town. Then he was good for a quick romp between the sheets.

He stood and stared at himself in the mirror on his closet door. Reaching up, Cal smoothed his hands over his tousled hair. He wasn't a bad-looking bloke. Though he didn't possess the charm and sophistication his two younger brothers did, he could show a girl a good time. And he could be romantic if required. That had to count for something, right?

As he jogged down the stairs, Cal turned his thoughts to the workday ahead. The month of June would be spent preparing for mustering, herding the cattle back into the station yards for inoculations, branding, tagging and sorting. From the first of July through the end of that month, every jackaroo on Kerry Creek Station would exist on caffeine, fifteen-minute meals and barely enough sleep to get them through a day's work.

The six station hands were already gathered around the table, devouring heaping platters of scrambled eggs, bacon, baked beans and toast. Mary hovered nearby, filling requests for coffee, juice and tea in her calm, efficient manner.

As he entered the room, the stockmen shouted their greetings. Cal took his place at the head of the table, observing the scene before him. Was it any wonder a woman would find station life unappealing? Table manners were all but nonexistent. Not a one of the stockmen had bothered to comb their hair that morning and he'd wager that most hadn't shaved in the past three days. What was the point when they all looked the same?

"I don't see why Miss Moynihan can't take her meals with us," Davey said, glancing around at his fellow jackaroos. "We can act polite." He snatched his serviette from his collar and laid it on his lap. "See?"

Cal reached for a piece of toast, then slathered it with strawberry jam. "Who is Miss Moynihan?"

"We have a guest," Mary said, setting a mug of coffee in front of him. She smoothed a strand of gray hair back into the tidy knot at the nape of her neck.

"We do?"

"Since you weren't here, I took it upon myself to offer her a place to stay. She's a genealogist come all the way from Dublin, Ireland, to do research on the Quinn family. She's been driving back and forth between here and Bilbarra for the past two days, waiting for you to get back."

"You invited a genealogist to stay at Kerry Creek?" Cal frowned. "What does she expect to find here?"

"She'd like to talk to you about Crevan Quinn, in particular. She's documented the Quinn line going all the way back to the ancient kings of Ireland. You ought to take a look at her work. It's all very interesting."

"Where did you put her?" Cal asked.

"She stayed in the south bunkhouse last night. She'll be driving back to Bilbarra to fetch her things this morning, if you approve. I don't think her research will take long."

"I'm not going to have time for her," Cal said, grabbing the platter of eggs and scooping a spoonful onto his plate. He sent Mary a shrewd look. "If you ask my opinion, I think you're happy to have another woman on Kerry Creek who will sip tea and eat biscuits with you all afternoon."

Mary gave his head a playful slap. "I'm the only one on Kerry Creek who has managed to maintain a bit of civility. Look at the lot of you, gobbling down your food like hogs at a trough. I'd wager you'd all act differently if we had a lady at the table."

"Oh, so you invited her to stay so we'd improve our manners?" Cal picked up his serviette and placed it daintily in his lap, holding out his little fingers as he did so. "Hear that, boys? Our Mary thinks we're all a bunch of uncouth cane toads."

"Can I tell her you'll meet with her after dinner tonight?"

"Let Brody or Teague take this one," Cal said wearily. "I've got far too much on my list."

"Brody took off for Bilbarra on Friday and hasn't been seen since and Teague has responsibilities with Doc Daley. He spent last night at Dunbar Station and isn't supposed to be back until later this morning."

The phone on the wall rang and Mary wiped her hands on her apron before picking it up. When she finished with the call, she sighed and shook her head.

"What is it?" Cal asked.

"That was Angus Embley. Your brother raised quite the stink in town last night. It appears Brody's lost his keys down the dunny at the Spotted Dog. Angus asked if someone could bring him a spare set and bail him out of jail."

"I'm not going," Cal said. "This is the third time in as many months."

"You will go," Mary said, her voice firm. Though she wasn't related to the Quinns, she had served as a surrogate mother ever since their own mother had left the station twelve years before. Cal recognized the tone of voice and knew not to argue.

Since Brody had arrived on Kerry Creek a few months ago, he'd been nothing but trouble. A motorcycle accident had ended his career as a pro footballer and Brody had found himself at loose ends, unable to deal with the loss of everything he'd worked for. Though he wasn't a pauper, the money he'd made wouldn't last forever. Sooner or later, Brody would have to make a decision about a new career. But for now, he'd been living off his notoriety and the patience and generosity of his oldest brother. But this had gone far enough.

"Teague probably has to fly into Bilbarra today. He can just—"

"You'll not leave your brother sitting in the nick," Mary scolded. "Besides, it will do you good to get off this station for a few hours. You can pick up supplies and the mail, and maybe even get yourself a decent haircut."

"All right, all right," Cal said. He pushed away from the table and stood, then snatched another piece of toast from a passing platter. "If I leave now, I'll be back before lunch."

Mary fetched her list and handed it to him. "Stop by the library, too, will you? Daisy called to tell me my books were in."

"Any other requests?" he asked, looking around the table.

"The windmill up in the northwest paddock is rattling," Skip said. "We should probably take it apart before mustering and replace the bearings."

"I'll order the parts," Cal said. He grabbed his stockman's hat from the peg near the door, then nodded to the men gathered around the table. "Comb your hair for once, will ya, boys? I'm sick to death of looking at you."

Cal jogged down the porch steps to his ute. He tucked Mary's list into his shirt pocket, then hopped behind the wheel. A cloud of dust billowed out behind him as he drove down the long dirt road.

Though the drive into Bilbarra took two hours, Cal had made it so many times in his life that he barely noticed the time passing. The closer he got to town, the smoother the roads became, though none of them were paved. He slipped a CD into the player and let his mind wander, thinking about his chances of finding a wife.

He'd always known his place was at Kerry Creek. From the time he was a boy, he'd carefully watched each element of the operation, taking on more and more responsibility with every year that passed. He'd never expected to be boss cocky before he turned thirty. But when his parents had decided to reconcile, his father had reluctantly handed the reins over to Cal and left for Sydney.

Cal imagined that Jack Quinn's decision had been made easier knowing the station was in good hands. And after his parents' last visit, he could see the choice had been right for them both. His mother taught school in Sydney and his father had started a small landscaping business. They'd bought a house near the ocean and were happy being together again.

As he turned east on the main road into Bilbarra, Cal squinted as the early-morning sun emerged at the top of a rise. He grabbed his sunglasses from the dashboard, but they fell to the floor of the ute. Bending down, he searched for them with his fingers. But when he glanced out the windshield again, Cal was startled to find himself heading directly toward a figure standing in the middle of the road.

GEMMA SAW THE TRUCK COMING toward her and frantically waved her arms above her head. She'd been stuck here, at the edge of nowhere, for nearly thirty minutes. Not a single living creature had happened by beyond a few hundred flies and a small, evil-looking lizard. But now, as the vehicle was coming closer, she realized the driver hadn't seen her—or he didn't intend to stop.

She shouted, jumping up and down to gain the driver's attention. For an instant, she thought he might run her down and she scurried to safety, but then suddenly, the truck veered sharply and drove off the edge of the road. It came to a dead stop when the front wheels hit the bottom of a shallow gully. Gemma held her breath, afraid to move, adrenaline coursing through her. She'd been the cause of this accident and now she wasn't sure what to do. Her mobile wasn't working and she was at least fifteen kilometers from Bilbarra and help.

"Oh, please, oh, please," she chanted as she raced over to the truck, climbing down into where it had come to rest. The driver's-side window was open and she could see a man inside. He was conscious and staring out the windscreen. "Are you all right?" she asked, coughing from the dust that hung in the air.

He turned and looked at her, then blinked vacantly. "Yes," he murmured. He closed his eyes, then opened them again, shaking his head. "Are you real? Or am I dead?"

His question caught her by surprise and she reached inside and grabbed his arm, then pinched it hard. "Do you feel that?"

"Ow!" He rubbed his skin, glaring at her.

"I'm very real. And you're fine. You haven't hit your head, have you? Are you bleeding anywhere?"

He reached up and pushed his hat off. The moment he did, Gemma got a good look at his face. She took a step back, a shiver skittering through her body. Suddenly breathless, she tried to inhale. But her lungs had ceased to function properly. She felt a bit dizzy and wondered if all that adrenaline was wearing off too quickly. Her fingers gripped the edge of the window as she tried to remain upright.

The driver pushed against the door with his shoulder and it swung open, sending her stumbling backward. "I'm so sorry," she said. Good Lord, he was absolutely the most gorgeous thing she'd ever seen in her life. Although Australia was teeming with beautiful men, Gemma felt quite certain that she'd hit the jackpot with this bloke.

He was fine, handsome without being pretty. His features, taken individually, were quite ordinary, but together they combined to make up a man of unquestionable masculinity, rugged and powerful and perhaps a tiny bit dangerous.

Gemma took another step back as he approached and her heel caught on a rock. An instant later, she landed on her bum, the impact causing her to cry out. Gemma felt something move beneath her hand and she looked down to see a lizard squirming between her fingers.

This time, it was a shriek that erupted from her lips as she scrambled to her feet to escape. But she lost her balance again and pitched forward into his arms. He held on to her until she was back on her feet, looking down at her in utter bewilderment.

"Is it poisonous?" she asked, frantically wiping her

hand on the front of his shirt. "Jaysus, I hate those things. They're slimy little buggers. Look, did he bite me?"

Her question seemed to shake him out of his stupor. "It's a gecko." He smiled crookedly. "I—I reckon you are real. I don't expect angels screech like that." He gradually loosened his grip on her arms. "I almost hit you, miss. What the hell were you doing in the middle of the road?"

"I was trying to wave you down," Gemma said. "I have a punctured tire. I've tried to change it myself, but I can't get the bloody things off. The…screws. The bolts. Didn't you see me?"

"Nuts," he said. "They're called nuts." He took her elbow and gently led her back to the road. "The sun was in my eyes." Drawing a deep breath, he surveyed the scene, his attention moving between his truck and her car. "Come on, I'll help you change it."

She looked back over her shoulder. "Shouldn't we get your truck back on the road first?"

"No worries," he said with a shrug. "It's not stuck." He walked up to the Subaru wagon she'd rented in Sydney and squatted down beside the flat.

Her attention was caught by the way his jeans hugged his backside. They fit him like a glove, not so tight that it looked like he was trying too hard to be sexy, but just tight enough to attract her notice.

Her eyes moved to his shoulders, and the muscles shifting and bunching beneath the faded work shirt. Then he stood and faced her. Gemma liked the way he moved, so easy, almost graceful.

"These roads around here are shite," he said, wiping

his hands on his jeans. "If you hit enough holes, a tire will go flat without a puncture."

Gemma pointed to the jack, lying in the dust. "I tried to change it myself, but I have no earthly clue what I'm doing. I was starting to get worried when no one came by."

"This road doesn't go many places," he said.

She stood over him as he put the jack together and hooked it beneath the front of the car. Watching him, Gemma realized she never would have figured out how to change the tire on her own. She bent down beside him. From this vantage point, she could get a better look at his face. He was deeply tanned and his eyes were an odd shade of hazel, more gold than green. "Thank you so very much for stopping."

"I didn't have much choice," he said. "It was that or run you down." He straightened and began to pump the handle. Slowly, the front end of the car rose. Then he started on the nuts that held the tire to the car.

As he worked, she studied him more closely. He wasn't much of a conversationalist. She'd always thought the strong, silent type was just a myth, but here was a man who proved it. He was tall, over six feet. His clothes were well-worn and she suspected he worked on one of the stations in the area. She made several more attempts to engage him, but he seemed intent on his task.

Since the weather and the flies hadn't sparked a discussion, she decided to try asking about places to eat in Bilbarra. He'd been headed in that direction and once he was through with her tire, she'd offer to buy him lunch.

Though Gemma had been anxious to get back to

Kerry Creek with her things, the Quinn brothers had been scarce. According to the housekeeper, Cal had been camping in the outback for a few days and Brody had stayed overnight in Bilbarra. She'd met Teague briefly on the morning she'd first arrived at the station, but he hadn't had time to talk. Since she wasn't getting anywhere with the Quinns, why not spend a little time with this stranger?

Her plan had seemed so simple back in Dublin. But now that she was here in Queensland, ready to play the part of a curious genealogist, Gemma was getting nervous. What if they didn't believe her? What if she tripped herself up and revealed her real reason for coming?

For a long time, she'd thought the Emerald of Eire had been nothing but an overblown legend, based more in fantasy than truth. Her mother had told her about it when she'd been little and it had piqued Gemma's imagination—not because of the jewel, but because it had something to do with Gemma's father, David Parnell.

Before the age of twelve, her father had been nothing more than a faded photo. But suddenly, Gemma realized she was part of something bigger, a family history.

According to her mother, the jewel had been stolen from Gemma's fourth great-grandfather, Lord Stanton Parnell, more than one hundred and fifty years ago. Some of the Parnells believed that with the loss of the emerald, the fortunes of the family had been cursed.

The fortunes of Orla Moynihan had definitely fallen the moment she set eyes on David Parnell. According to her mother, they'd fallen in love instantly. David had promised to find the emerald so they might run away together and get married. Gemma suspected this was only a ploy to lure her mother into his bed. A pregnancy followed and David disappeared, behind the protective walls of the Parnell family estate. The baby was named Gemma, after an emerald and a dream.

It was no surprise that David had abandoned her mother. The Parnells were part of the old English aristocracy that had made their fortunes in the Belfast textile industry. And Parnell sons didn't marry poor Irish girls, no matter what the circumstances.

Gemma had met her father twice, once when she'd barged into his office on her twelfth birthday and the other on the day she'd turned eighteen, when she'd demanded he pay for her university tuition at University College in Dublin. He had his own family, including a wife not ten years older than Gemma, so he had sent her away with a promise. He would pay if she'd never approach him again.

But throughout her childhood, Gemma had dreamed of someday being part of that family, of living in a posh house, of having servants to wait on her, of never having to worry about whether they could afford to pay the rent that month. And the emerald had come to represent that dream, something precious and beautiful.

Finding the Emerald of Eire was her chance to claim her birthright. Whether it fixed things with the Parnells or she just threw it in her father's face, it would prove that she had Parnell blood running through her veins, even though it had been tainted by the Irish of the Moynihans.

So she'd gone to university, thanks to the Parnell scholarship. Gemma had focused her studies on medieval Irish history and after receiving her doctorate, she'd been offered a teaching position. One day, last year, while researching an article on medieval prisons, she'd decided to see if there was any truth to the family legend. To her astonishment, everything her mother had told her was there—the emerald, the theft, the trial of the pickpocket, Crevan Quinn.

Yes, there had been an Emerald of Eire, a 72-carat jewel that Stanton Parnell had bought in Europe to give to his young bride. He'd been carrying it in his coat pocket on the streets of Dublin in February of 1848 when a local pickpocket had stolen it. Though Crevan Quinn had been tried and later shipped off to Australia for his crime, the jewel had never been recovered.

Even now, she imagined the headlines in the papers, the proof in black and white that Gemma Moynihan, illegitimate daughter of David Parnell, was an heir to the Parnell millions. Though her mother refused to ask for a DNA test, the emerald would be Gemma's bargaining chip. If they wanted it back, then David would have to acknowledge her as his daughter.

She'd completed her research in six months and was armed with a list of leads, all of which led her to Australia and the descendants of Crevan Quinn. One didn't possess a jewel like that without either selling it or passing it down as an heirloom. And since an emerald that size would have caused some notice had it been sold, it was probably still in the Quinn's possession.

"Can you hold these?"

Gemma brushed a strand of hair out of her eyes, startled back to reality by the stranger's voice. He handed her the nuts. "That was quick. I don't think I'd ever have been able to get those off on my own. I—I hope I'm not keeping you from anything," she said.

"Nothing important." He stood and wiped his hands on his jeans, then walked to the tailgate to retrieve the spare. "You should get the tire repaired straight away. You don't want to get stranded out here again without a spare." He shoved the spare onto the bolts and she handed him the nuts, one by one.

"Good advice," she murmured.

"You're from Ireland." He looked at her again, this time with a rather odd expression. "Are you here for a visit?"

It was the closest they'd come to a two-sided conversation and Gemma jumped at the chance. She was known to be quite charming, with a ready wit. But she hadn't had a chance to prove herself with this man. "I am. I'm staying out at Kerry Creek Station. Do you know it?"

She saw his shoulders stiffen. "Is that where you're headed now?"

She nodded. "And you? Do you live out here or in town?"

He pointed off toward the west. "Right out there, beyond the black stump. In the back of nowhere."

Well, if she wanted to find him, it wasn't going to be easy with those directions. Was the black stump a local landmark, or just another Aussie saying? For such a gorgeous man, he was impossible to flirt with.

Gemma stared down at his back as he let the car down with the jack, fascinated by the way his dark hair curled around his collar and his muscles flexed beneath the fabric of his shirt. Her fingers twitched as she fought the urge to touch him again. She held her breath in an effort to focus her mind.

When he'd finished, he bolted the flat to the rack on the tailgate and tossed the jack inside. "There you go," he said, wiping his hands on his jeans. "Good as new. Or almost."

"You must let me pay you," Gemma insisted. "Or let me treat you to lunch. There's a lovely coffee shop in town. They make the best meat pies."

"No, thank you," he said. "I'm happy to oblige, miss." He hesitated and she was certain he was about to change his mind, but then he moved toward his truck. "G'day, miss. Drive safe." He gave her a quick tip of his hat and walked away. She watched as he hopped inside, then slowly backed the truck out of the gully and onto the road. As he drove off toward town, Gemma stared after him.

She pressed her hand to her chest, her heart beating furiously beneath her fingertips. "Idiot," she muttered. She'd made a botch of that. All the other men she'd met here in Australia had seemed to like her. He was probably involved, or married. Or not attracted to her in the least. Maybe Australian men didn't fancy pale Irish girls with red hair and small breasts.

Besides, not all white knights were supposed to fall in love with their damsels in distress. It was a historical fact. Once she got back to Dublin, she'd research it thoroughly and write a paper. Gemma smiled to herself.

Whenever she found herself faced with a dilemma, it always helped to put it in historical context.

"I SAID I WAS SORRY."

Cal stared at the toes of his boots as his brother apologized. Though he knew he ought to kick Brody's arse for his behavior, he was tired of being his brother's keeper. If Brody wanted to stuff up his life, then that was his choice. Cal was much more interested in thinking about the woman he'd met on the road.

Gemma Moynihan. When Mary had mentioned her, he'd assumed the genealogist would be older, a granny sort with gray hair and glasses. Instead, she was stunningly beautiful, with flawless skin and a riot of auburn hair that fell in waves around her face. Though she looked quite young, Cal guessed she was probably about his age, give or take a few years on either side.

From the moment he heard her speak, in that lilting Irish accent, Cal had wondered if she was the one. And when he learned her name, he thought of introducing himself right then and there. But she'd already left him tongue-tied and he didn't want to make a fool of himself right off. He needed time to gather his wits about him.

It had taken him the entire ride into town to calm his racing pulse and consider what their encounter had meant. Though he'd maintained his calm while speaking to her, it had taken a tremendous effort not to stare at her, to analyze her every word and to fantasize about what she'd look like naked.

He rubbed his hands together, remembering the feel of her silken skin beneath his fingertips. Would he have another chance with her? Or would things change when she found out who he really was? Suddenly, he wanted to get out of Bilbarra and return to the station to find out.

"You're turning into a fair wanker, you are," Cal muttered. "You could find something better to do with yourself. Like lending a hand on the station. We could use your help mustering now that Teague's practice is starting to take off. He's been taking calls almost every day. And when he's home, he spends his time doing paperwork."

"I haven't decided what I'm going to do," Brody replied. "But it bloody well doesn't include stockman's work. Now, can I have my keys? I've got some place to go."

Cal reached in his jacket pocket for the spare key to his brother's Land Rover. "Buddy doesn't want you back at the Spotted Dog. You're going to have to find yourself another place to get pissed. Or you could give up the coldies. It would save you some money." Cal patted his brother on the shoulder. "I'm sorry things didn't turn out the way you wanted them to. Sometimes life is just crap. But you pick yourself up and you get on with it. And you stop being such a dickhead."

Brody gave his brother a shove, then stood up. "Give it a rest. If I needed a mother, I'd move back to Sydney and live with the one I already have."

Brody snatched his keys from Cal's hand, then jogged down the front steps and out into the dusty street. "I'll catch you later."

Cal watched him stride toward the Spotted Dog. He

heard the screen door of the police station creak and Angus Embley, the town police chief, stepped outside.

"How much trouble did he make?" Cal asked.

"Nothing too serious. Just a broken mirror."

"Well, if he can't drink at the Spotted Dog, he's going to have to drive halfway to Brisbane to find another pub."

"Give the boy a break, Cal," Angus said. "It's got to be an adjustment coming back here after all that time away."

Cal slowly stood and adjusted the brim of his hat. "Thanks for taking him in, Angus. I don't like the thought of him driving back to the station when he's pissed. It's good to know he has a place to sleep it off."

"No worries," Angus said with a nod.

Cal walked back to his ute and jumped inside. Though he had Mary's grocery list in his pocket and orders to stop for the mail and her library books, he was tempted to head right back to Kerry Creek.

It felt odd to be preoccupied with thoughts of a woman. Running a successful cattle station usually consumed all his attention. But there were times when Cal worried needlessly over business because there was nothing else in his life to think about. The genealogist was worth additional consideration.

He steered the ute towards the post office. Many of the outback stations got their mail by plane, but Teague and Brody spent enough time in town that they usually picked it up and brought it home, saving the mail plane a trip.

He grabbed a stack of letters from Mel Callahan, the seventy-five-year-old clerk, then returned to his ute. But one of the envelopes caught his eye and he stopped to open it. "You have been matched with three lovely mates," he murmured, reading the note inside. He flipped through the three photos, then continued reading. "To learn more, visit their profiles on the Outback-Mates Web site."

He looked at the three candidates again, studying them carefully. There wasn't one who came close to Gemma Moynihan's beauty, though they were all quite pretty by anyone's standards. But there was something about the Irish girl he found compelling, something that made him want to get to know her a lot better…and more intimately.

"Sorry, ladies." Cal jumped back into the pickup, then opened the glove box and shoved the envelope inside. For now, he was taking himself off the menu. As long as Gemma was staying at Kerry Creek, he'd focus his modest charms on her. After all, what did he have to lose? She was beautiful, intriguing and close at hand, three qualities that he found irresistible.

Cal reached for the key, then stopped. What if he fell in love with her? Still, that wasn't likely. He'd never been in love before, so he probably wouldn't know it if it dropped out of the sky and hit him on the noggin. But he did know about lust. And his feelings for Gemma were definitely of the lustful variety.

After she left Kerry Creek, he'd get back to his search for a wife. Cal pulled out onto the street and headed out of Bilbarra toward the station, the groceries forgotten. Unfortunately, the ride dragged on forever. He'd covered the distance between the station and town so many times it had become second nature. He knew all the landmarks and could probably find his way home blindfolded. But now that he had something important to do, every kilometer passed at a grindingly slow pace.

By the time he pulled into the yard, Cal figured he was about an hour behind Gemma. It was nearly time for lunch and if he was lucky, he'd find her sitting at the kitchen table with Mary. He took the steps two at a time and pulled the screen door open. But the kitchen was empty.

A huge pot of mutton stew bubbled on the stove and Mary had freshly baked bread to go with it. Cal decided to use the extra time to clean up. He hung his hat on the peg, then strode through the house to the stairs. He met Mary coming down.

"Oh, wonderful. You're back. I'm almost out of coffee and I need yeast to—"

"I didn't get supplies," Cal said. "Sorry. We'll call Teague. He can pick them up when he's in town today. Where is Gemma Moynihan?"

Mary gave him an odd look. "She's in the bunkhouse unpacking her things. She drove into town at dawn to get them. She said she had a flat tire on her way back to the station but some bloke stopped and changed it for her."

"Yes. That was me," he said.

"So you met her?" Mary asked.

"Not properly. Why didn't you tell me she was… you know."

"Young?"

"Pretty," he said.

"I thought you'd find out soon enough."

"Did you invite her to lunch?" Cal asked.

"I told her I'd take her out something to eat after the boys were fed."

"Leave that to me," he said. "I'm just going to change and I'll be right down."

He ran up the stairs and into his room, stripping off his shirt along the way. Though he'd taken a shower before breakfast, he figured another wouldn't hurt. The road had been dusty and his hair was sticking up all willy-nilly. He only had one chance to make a first impression—or a second impression.

He managed a shower in less than five minutes, then grabbed a towel for his wet hair. Luckily, he'd taken the time to shave off three days of stubble that morning. A splash of cologne was probably overkill, so he set the bottle back on the shelf.

Cal stepped into the hallway, rubbing his head with the towel until his hair was barely damp. But when he pulled the towel away, he found Gemma standing next to the linen closet, a blanket clutched to her chest, her eyes wide. A tiny cry of surprise slipped from her lips as the blanket dropped to the floor.

They both bent to pick it up, Cal getting to it first. He held it out to her as he rose. Gemma straightened, her gaze drifting along his naked body. He struggled to wrap the towel around his waist, but with only one hand, it was impossible to do. It seemed like an eternity before she took the blanket from him.

A long embarrassed silence followed as he tried to come up with a clever line. Of all the scenarios he'd gone over in his mind, this was not the way he'd intended their first meeting to go—him starkers and her all fascinated with his bits and pieces. Cal swallowed hard, realizing there was only one thing to say. "Hello," he said.

Her gaze quickly returned to his face and a pretty blush stained her cheeks. "Wha-what are you doing here?"

"I live here," he said. Though this wasn't exactly the way he wanted it to go, he'd have to make the best of it. "I'm Callum Quinn. Cal."

Stunned, she slowly took his outstretched hand, her fingers soft against his palm. "I'm—"

"Gemma Moynihan," he said. "I know. The genealogist. Mary told me."

She frowned, shaking her head in confusion. "But why didn't you introduce yourself on the road?"

"I didn't realize who you were at first. I thought you'd be older—I mean, I just assumed. Mary didn't say that you—weren't. Older."

She looked around, as if searching for the quickest means of escape. "I—I should let you get dressed. Mary just sent me up to fetch another blanket for the bunkhouse."

"I'm sure she did," he muttered, wondering at the housekeeper's motives. "I'll see you later?"

Gemma nodded. "Right. Later, then. All right." She turned and hurried back to the stairs, looking over her shoulder once before descending. Cal listened as her footfalls echoed from the lower hallway, then leaned back against the wall.

He'd always been the one who'd struggled to speak

around women. It was obvious his lack of clothing had something to do with her unease. Maybe that was the key with this woman? To shed his clothes as quickly as possible whenever the conversation slowed so neither one of them would have to talk?

Fate had dropped Gemma Moynihan into the middle of the outback and he was going to make the best of the opportunity. In reality, she was trapped here, waiting for him to enlighten her about his family history. He'd dole out a few interesting tidbits here and there, just enough to keep her around long enough for him to explore this attraction between them.

But the first thing he'd do was make it clear to every man on Kerry Creek Station, including his two brothers, that Gemma was off-limits. Though he knew she wouldn't be staying long, he could use the practice. When the right woman did present herself, he wanted to be ready.

"Lunch," he murmured. He'd get Mary to make up something for them both and then he'd take her on a tour of the station. The more time they spent alone, the better his chances of charming her. And if that didn't work, he'd just strip down and tempt her with his other attributes.

2

GEMMA RACED DOWN THE STAIRS, her face hot, her pulse pounding. She stopped at the bottom, grasping the newel post and drawing a deep breath. Had she just imagined that entire encounter? She'd spent the drive to Kerry Creek mentally undressing the man she'd met on the road, trying to conjure an image of him without his clothes. Was it any wonder that all came back when she met him again?

"No," she murmured. He had definitely been naked. She had imagined a good body beneath those clothes, but nothing quite as perfect as what she'd seen upstairs. She took a ragged breath, then continued on to the kitchen, desperate to return to the bunkhouse where she could enjoy her embarrassment in solitude.

"Did you find it?" Mary asked as Gemma hurried through the kitchen.

"Yes, thank you," Gemma called, shoving the screen door open with her free hand.

Some of the ranch hands were coming in for lunch and they watched her with unabashed interest as she passed. She wondered if her face was as red as it felt. It wasn't like she'd never seen a naked man before. She had—many times. But what had ever possessed her to stare in such a blatant way?

Gemma walked inside the bunkhouse, then slammed the door behind her. Crossing to the bed, she flopped onto it, facedown into the pillow. An image of Cal flashed in her mind again. Oh, God. He had an incredible body, from top to toe, and the all the interesting parts in between. She groaned again. Yes, there, too.

"Be careful what you wish for," Gemma said as she rolled onto her back. From the moment he'd driven off, she'd regretted not being more aggressive. She had always been the one in control of a relationship. She'd decided when it began and when it ended.

Similarly, she'd decided she wanted the post as senior instructor at University College, and had convinced the entire department that, even at her young age, she was the perfect person for the job. Her article on Irish religious icons made the cover of the university's history journal, because she'd decided that was where it belonged. And when they'd demanded that she teach during the summer, she'd convinced them that her time would be much better spent doing research for a new book.

But here, she'd seen something she wanted—a man—and she was suddenly afraid to go after him. A summer romance was exactly what she needed, even though it was technically a winter romance here in Australia. It had been months since she'd been with a man. Yet, it didn't seem quite ethical.

She was here to extract information from Cal. If

they had a physical relationship at the same time, wouldn't she be using her body to further her agenda? Gemma pinched her eyes shut. Wasn't that what sex was about? Most women had an agenda—first sex, then marriage, a comfortable life, a good future. Her plan was just a wee bit different.

But if he knew what she was here for, then she wouldn't be deceiving anyone. An emerald worth a half million English pounds wasn't something he'd just turn over, simply because she said it belonged to her family. And if she found proof of the sale of the stone, then she could demand he return the ill-gotten profits.

The more Gemma became involved in her scheme, the more she realized how complicated things could become. But a few nights of brilliant sex was nothing compared to assuring her identity as a Parnell. She'd wanted Cal Quinn's body for about three hours. She'd wanted to be a Parnell for years.

Gemma had always been so practical about sex. The physical release was enjoyable but she'd carefully avoided emotional attachments. Though there had been a number of lovers in her life, she'd never been in love. Watching her mother gradually destroy herself over a man she couldn't have was enough to make Gemma cautious.

A knock sounded on the bunkhouse door and she sat up, tossing her hair over her shoulder. Gemma weighed the chances that Cal was on the other side. How could she face him without thinking about his naked—? She groaned as the knock grew more insistent.

"Come in," she called.

The door swung open and Mary walked in with a

tray. "Hello, there. I've brought you some lunch. Just a sandwich and some crisps. And a lovely slice of apple pie." She set it down on the table near the door. "The boys are having stew, but I thought you'd prefer this. What would you care to drink? We have beer, lemonade and wine. There's even milk, if you prefer that."

"Lemonade is fine, thanks. But you don't have to wait on me. I'll come in."

"No, no, I'll send Cal out with it. You two can meet—again."

Gemma covered her face with her hands. "Oh, Jaysus, he told you about that?" She shook her head and peeked between her fingers at the housekeeper. "He startled me and I didn't know what to do or where to look. One isn't often confronted with a naked man."

Mary gasped. "Naked? What was he doing driving around in the nuddy?"

"Driving?" She paused, then smiled. "Oh, no. I'm not talking about the first time we met. I'm talking about the second time. Upstairs. He was coming out of the bath and I was—"

"Oh dear," Mary said, a look of horror on her face. "Oh, I am so sorry. He said he was going up to change his clothes. I just assumed he'd come down and gone outside." Flustered, the housekeeper began to rearrange the lunch on the table.

"Don't worry," Gemma said, crossing the room to stand beside her. "It's not like I didn't enjoy the view. He is quite fetching in the nip."

Mary glanced over at her, then laughed. "I see you'll fit in just fine around here. Living with all these men takes a certain amount of tolerance. That's why I think it best you work your way up to meals in the kitchen. Their behavior can be bawdy and their language a little raw."

"I'm Irish. We invented bawdy," she said.

"Well, then, we'll see you at dinner. And I'll just go get that lemonade."

Gemma pulled on her cardie and grabbed her sandwich and crisps, following Mary out onto the porch. The winter weather in Queensland was much warmer than winter in Dublin, pleasant enough to eat lunch alfresco. She plopped down on the top step and set her plate beside her. The sandwich was huge—a thick slab of warm ham between two slices of home-made bread. Mary had added mustard, remembering that Gemma had liked it from their lunch the day before.

Gemma had left so early for Bilbarra that she hadn't bothered with breakfast. Famished, she took a huge bite of the sandwich and sighed. Food tasted so much better here. Maybe it was because someone more competent than herself was doing the cooking.

She heard the screen door slam and Gemma looked up to see Cal striding across the yard, a glass of lemonade in his hand. She chewed furiously and managed to swallow right before he stopped in front of her. "Hi," she croaked, pasting a bright smile on her face.

"Mary sent this out."

Gemma took it from his outstretched hand, avoiding his gaze. "Thanks."

He rocked back on his heels and nodded, his hands shoved in his jean pockets. "Well, enjoy your lunch."

"Would you care to join me?" Gemma asked. "This sandwich is big enough for the both of us."

Cal thought about her offer for a long moment, then shrugged. "Sure. But first, I want to apologize for—"

"Oh, no," Gemma interrupted. "You don't have to— It was my— I didn't mind." She laughed nervously. "I mean, it didn't bother me. I have seen a man naked before. Several times. More than several. Many." She winced. "Not that many. Enough."

"And you'd rather not see any more?"

"No," she said. "Yes. I'd rather not be surprised by one. But I don't mind…looking." Gemma took another bite of her sandwich. She wasn't having much luck using her mouth to speak. Perhaps she ought to stick to chewing.

"Mary said you wanted to talk to me about our family history."

"I do."

"Why?"

She'd expected the question and had a story all worked out. "Because I'm interested in what happened after your ancestors left Ireland. I'm working on a book. On the Quinn family."

"Why the Quinns?" he asked.

"Because a Quinn is paying me to do the research," she lied. "Edwin Quinn. He's a very important man. And he wants to know more about his family." She held her breath, waiting for him to either question her further or accept the story as it was.

"Why would someone pay to know all that? All those people are dead. That's the past. Aren't you more interested in the present?"

"I'm a historian. We're supposed to be interested in the past," Gemma explained. "And I think dead people can be very interesting. Did you know your third great-grandfather, Crevan Quinn, came to Australia on a convict ship?"

He nodded. "Most of the early settlers in Australia did. He was a thief. A pickpocket. He served his time and his parole in New South Wales and after that, he was a free man. He came up to Queensland and worked hard, bought some land and started Kerry Creek." He took a bite of his half of the sandwich. "There's a painting of him in the front parlor."

"I'd like to see that," Gemma said.

"I'll take you on a tour of the station, if you like. Although there are more interesting things to see than that old painting."

She looked over at him and noticed that he had a bit of mustard on his lower lip. Without thinking, Gemma reached out and wiped it away with her finger. But then, she wasn't sure what to do with it. "Mustard," she murmured.

He took her hand and pulled her finger to his lips, then licked the yellow blob from the tip. It was such a silly thing, but Gemma felt a flood of heat race through her body. She drew a quick breath, desperate to maintain her composure.

Cal didn't seem to be faring much better. He quickly let loose of her hand. She picked up the lemonade and took a gulp, hoping to break the tension. But the drink was more tart than she expected and it went down the wrong way. The more Gemma coughed, the worse it became and before long, her eyes were watering.

"Are you all right? Are you choking?"

He smoothed his hand over her back, gently patting. But his touch only made her more uncomfortable. She imagined his hands moving to her face, to her breasts, to her— "Oh," she groaned.

"Here, take another drink," he said, holding the glass in front of her.

She waved him off, knowing that lemonade was the last thing she needed. Was there a reason she made a fool of herself every time he came near? When she'd finally regained control, she stared up at him through her tears, her gaze fixing on his mouth. He had such a nice mouth, Gemma mused.

And then, as if the humiliation wasn't enough, she leaned forward and pressed her lips to his. The kiss took him by surprise and he drew back, a startled expression on his face. Had she made a mistake? Had she misread the attraction between them?

Gemma cleared her throat. "Sorry. I have no idea why I did that." She paused, searching for a plausible excuse. "I wanted to thank you. For everything. Helping me on the road, giving me a place to stay. Talking to me about your family. That's all."

"No worries," he murmured. Cal drew a deep breath, his lips still inches from hers. "So, what about that tour?"

His breath was warm on her mouth and Gemma knew if she leaned forward, it would happen again. And this time, it would be better, because it wouldn't be a surprise to either one of them. "Now? I'd like to get started on my research if possible. Mary said you have some old family records in your library?"

"Sure. She can show you. We'll get together later. This evening. After dinner?"

"Mary invited me to join everyone in the kitchen. You'll be there, won't you?"

He nodded.

"Then we'll go after we eat. It's a date." Oh, she hadn't meant to say that. "It's a plan," she corrected. "A good plan."

The sound of an approaching car caught Cal's attention and he turned to watch a Land Rover drive into the yard. A soft curse slipped from his lips.

"Who is that?" she asked.

"My brother, Brody." Cal slowly stood as Brody hopped out of the car and ran around to the passenger side. A woman stepped out and Brody walked with her to the back door.

"It looks like he's brought another guest," she said. "Is that his girlfriend?"

Cal forced a smile. "I have to go. But I'll see you later."

He held out his hand, then drew it back. A handshake didn't seem right now that they'd kissed, Gemma mused. But what would be a proper way to part? She stood up and pressed her hand to his chest. He stared down at her fingers as she smoothed the faded fabric of his shirt. "I'll see you later."

Cal hesitated, before nodding, then jogging down the steps. Gemma rubbed her arms, trying to banish the shiver of excitement she felt. Cal Quinn wasn't like anyone she'd ever met. She'd always dated older men—at least ten years older. Men who had been sophisticated and highly educated, who spent their days thinking, not doing. Gemma had always assumed she'd been looking for that father figure she'd lacked in her life.

But Cal was nothing at all like her father—or like the men she'd dated. He was young and strong and undeniably sexy. Was she willing to put aside her quest to gain a father for a chance at a different kind of lover, a man who made her heart race and her knees wobble?

Gemma sat back down and picked up her sandwich. "I'll just have to separate my personal life from my…personal life." And deal with the consequences later.

CAL OPENED THE SCREEN DOOR and stepped inside the kitchen. The scent of Mary's pot roast hung in the air and she stood at the stove, making gravy from the pan drippings. He looked at the clock. Dinner began in exactly five minutes. Promptness at meal times was one of the only rules that Mary enforced at the station. But Cal was dirty and sweaty from working all day and he needed time to get cleaned up before he saw Gemma again.

He'd spent the day repairing the gates in the homestead yards where they'd driven the cattle after mustering. Focusing on the task had been difficult—his thoughts had been occupied with Gemma and the kiss they'd shared.

He hadn't been at all happy with his side of the encounter. The contact had stunned him, causing him to draw away instead of pulling her into his arms. Now, the only way to fix his mistake was to kiss her again. But Cal wasn't sure whether he ought to take the lead on that or let her make the first move again.

He hung his hat next to the door and rolled up his sleeves. "How long?" he asked.

"Look at the clock, Callum Quinn. Five minutes," Mary said. "Wash your hands and take a seat."

"I just thought I'd run up and catch a quick shower. Maybe you could hold off a bit?"

Mary turned, bracing her hands on her ample hips. "You can shower after dinner. The boys will want to eat and if you're not here when I put the food down, there won't be anything left." She turned off the flame on the stove, then pulled the gravy jug from the shelf above the sink. "You look just fine. Don't worry. You could be covered in mud and you'd still be a beaut."

"I'm not worried," Cal said. "What would I be worried about? Do you think I—?"

"Of course not. Sit."

Cal reluctantly took his place at the head of the table and Mary set a beer in front of him. He took a long drink and then leaned back in his chair. After his surprising lunch with Gemma, he'd gone on to have a very strange day.

Brody had brought home a stray girl he'd found living at the jail and had offered her a job working in the stables. Though Payton Harwell didn't look as though she'd done a hard day's work in her life, the stables had been spotless when he walked through a few hours later. Either she was efficient and tireless, or she'd managed to convince one of the jackaroos to help her.

Teague had shown up shortly after Payton's arrival, staying long enough to chat up both of the ladies. But then a call from Doc Daley had sent him off on an emergency visit in his SUV.

With his competition occupied, Cal was anxious to have Gemma to himself. But he had to get through dinner first. "Maybe I should let Gemma know that dinner's ready," he said, shoving his chair back.

"She knows. She spent the afternoon in the library and just went back to the bunkhouse a few minutes ago." Mary handed him a basket full of sliced bread. "Make yourself useful. Make a pot of coffee."

The six stockmen that worked Kerry Creek arrived at the back door, a boisterous group ready for a good meal and a few cold beers. "She's a bit of alright, I'd say," Skip Thompson said as he walked inside. He tossed his hat at the hooks on the wall, but it fell to the floor.

"That she is," Jack commented. "I like long hair. And long legs. What do you think, Cal?"

"About what?" Cal filled the filter with ground coffee and closed it, then flipped the switch.

"The Yank or the Irish lass? Which do you fancy?"

"I haven't thought about it," he lied.

"Ha!" Davey Thompson cried. "A little slow off the mark there, boss? Jack here has already decided to marry the Irish girl. He wants to get to making babies straight off."

Cal's jaw clenched. "I'll warn you yobbos to mind your manners. You'll not treat these women like the girls you play with at the Spotted Dog." A knock sounded on the door and he circled the table, pulling a serviette from out of Jack's collar. "On your lap," he muttered. "And no talking with your mouth full. No cursing. Or belching. Or farting."

He found Gemma waiting on the porch, dressed in a pretty blouse and blue jeans. "There's no need to knock," he said as he opened the door for her. She'd tied her hair back in a scarf and as she passed, he fought the temptation to pull it off and let her hair fall free.

It had been a long while since he'd enjoyed the pleasures of a woman's body and the scent of her was enough to make his blood warm. Now, presented with the perfect female form, he couldn't decide how to proceed. He placed his hand at the small of her back, steering her toward his end of the table.

Cal forced himself to breathe as the warmth from her body seeped into his fingers. This was crazy. Women may have been a bit scarce lately, but he'd always been able to control his desires. Just touching her was enough to send his senses into overdrive.

"Hello," she said, smiling at the boys seated at the table. Skip suddenly stood and the rest of the stockmen followed suit in a noisy clamor. "I'm Gemma."

Cal cleared his throat. He should be making the introductions. After all, she was technically his guest. "Gemma, that's Skip Thompson, and his younger brother, Davey. This is Jack Danbury. Over there is Mick Fermoy, Eddie Franklin and Pudge Bell. And you know Mary."

He waved Pudge out of the seat next to his and pulled

out the chair for Gemma. "It's nice to meet you," she said as she sat down, sending them all a dazzling smile.

The screen door slammed and Brody stepped inside, pulling his gloves off as he crossed the kitchen. He looked around the table at the boys, all still standing uncomfortably, before resting his sights on Gemma. A slow grin spread across his face as he approached.

"I'm Gemma Moynihan," she said in a lilting Irish accent. "And you must be Brody. I can see the family resemblance."

"Gemma," Brody repeated. He glanced over at Cal, an amused expression on his face. Was it that evident, this attraction he had to Gemma? Cal felt as if he had a sign around his neck—I Fancy The Irish Girl. Well, stiff bickies. If Brody could have his fun with Payton Harwell, then Cal would enjoy Gemma's visit, as well.

"Have you met Payton?" Brody asked, smiling warmly at Gemma.

"Yes, I did," Gemma said.

"Is she coming in to eat?" he asked.

"I don't know. She was lying in her bunk when I left. She looked knackered."

"Maybe I should take her something," Brody suggested, stepping away from the table. He grabbed a plate and loaded it with beef and potatoes, covering the entire meal with a portion of Mary's gravy. After fetching a couple beers from the fridge, he headed back out the door.

"Oh, ho," Mick said with a laugh. "If Brody doesn't go back to footie, Miss Shelly might give him a job as a waitress. I reckon he'd look real fetching in the apron."

The boys found the joke hilarious and they all sat back down and began passing around the platters and bowls that Mary set in front of them. Cal held the boiled potatoes out in front of Gemma. "If you want something else, I'm sure Mary could make it for you."

Gemma met his gaze and for a moment, Cal felt as if he couldn't move. Her eyes were the most incredible shade of green. And her lips were soft and lush, a perfect bow shape. If they'd been alone, he would have kissed her right then and there.

"This is fine," she said, smiling. "In Ireland, we love our praities. And I'm so hungry, I'd eat them ten ways."

She scooped a spoonful onto her plate, then took the bowl from his hands. Her fingers brushed his, but he didn't pull away. Though it was silly to crave such innocent contact, for now it was as close as he'd get to her.

"So where did you come from in Ireland?" Mick asked.

"Dublin," she said. "I teach at University College and my mother lives there. Though the Moynihans are originally from County Clare." She paused. "And my father lives in Belfast." The last she said so softly that only Cal could hear.

"My grandparents were from Ireland," Mick commented. "They came here right after they married."

"So you're the full quid, eh?" Jack said. Cal shot him a look and Jack shrugged. "She must be smart if she teaches at university."

"I hated history in school," Skip said. "Could never remember all those dates."

"It's not just about dates," Gemma said. "It's about life. What our lives are built upon. My grandfather loved history and I'd stay with him during the summer months. He had a library full of books and I think I must have read them all. I loved the stories of the ancient Irish kings and queens."

"I sure would have studied harder if my teacher looked like you," Skip said.

Cal glanced around the table to find each of the stockmen watching Gemma intently. "You're pretty enough to be a princess," Pudge said. The rest of the boys agreed and Pudge blushed.

"The Quinns are descended from the ancient kings," she said, glancing at Cal. "I've come here to trace the history of the Australian branch of the Quinn family. I'm hoping I can convince Cal to let me dig up all the family secrets."

She was teasing him and Cal wasn't sure how to react. He barely knew her. But he did know one thing about himself—he wasn't considered a very comical fella. Among the Quinn brothers, Cal was the serious one, the guy everybody could depend upon. Brody and Teague led much more interesting lives and probably had a helluva lot more secrets to tell.

"Do you have any secrets I should know about?" Gemma asked, a coy smile playing at her lips.

"Oh, no," Davey interrupted. "Cal's life is an open book."

"I think you saw all my secrets earlier," Cal muttered. As soon as he made the comment he wanted to take it back. It was a feeble attempt at humor. It hadn't been the most proper of introductions and he probably should have just let the memory fade.

He did have a few secrets, though. He hadn't told anyone about the matchmaking service. And he'd been perving over the genealogist since he'd met her, spending most of the day trying to figure a way he might act upon his desires. *That* would go over big if he said it out loud.

"I have a secret," Davey volunteered. "And I'm not mingy about keeping it."

"Yeah," Skip said. "Davey's big secret is that he still sleeps with a teddy bear."

The rest of the jackaroos burst out laughing and Davey turned five shades of red. "I—I do not."

"I think that's nice," Gemma said. "I have a little monkey that sleeps on my bed. My grandmother gave him to me when I was young. He's made from one of my grandfather's socks and he's still one of my most precious possessions."

Davey looked around the table, a smug smile on his face. "See?"

The boys fell silent and Cal watched Gemma silently. She had a kind heart. It would have been easy to get caught up in the teasing, but she'd sensed that Davey would have been embarrassed, so she put a stop to it by siding with him.

Though he'd only known her for part of a day, Cal couldn't help but be curious about the attraction. It wasn't just physical. Yes, he thought she was beautiful. But there was more to this than just lust. Besides wanting to take her to bed, he also wanted to sit down and learn everything he could about her.

Who was she? What was her life like in Ireland? Did

she have a whole stable full of blokes just waiting to romance her or had she found a man to love? Though they weren't proper questions to ask a near stranger who was only interested in his family tree, he wanted to believe they'd move past the professional and into something much more personal the moment they were alone again. After all, she had seen him naked. That was pretty personal.

The remainder of the dinner passed in polite conversation. The boys peppered her with question after question just to keep her talking. By the end of the meal, they'd all fallen madly in love with her. When she set her serviette next to her plate and excused herself from the table, they all jumped to their feet to help with her chair.

Cal followed her out the door. Though he wanted to appear indifferent, he suspected that his preference was quite clear to everyone at the table. Was he making a fool of himself? To a casual observer, Gemma might appear to be seriously out of his league. Smart, sophisticated, beautiful. But she'd been the one to kiss him first. Maybe he did have a chance.

In truth, a part of him wanted her to finish her business and leave as quickly as possible. Her presence at Kerry Creek had upset his well-ordered life. But another part of him wanted the luxury of time—as long as it would take before he'd feel comfortable enough to touch her again, to kiss her, to make— "So, would you like that tour now?" he asked, pushing the thoughts from his head.

Gemma nodded. "Sure. I'm just going to grab my cardie from the bunkhouse and I'll be right back."

"All right," Cal said. "I'll be here. Waiting."

He watched her walk across the yard, fascinated by the gentle sway of her hips. It was nice to have a woman close at hand, to be able to enjoy looking at her whenever he chose. It may not last long, but he'd damn well enjoy it while he could.

GEMMA STEPPED BACK OUT onto the porch of the bunkhouse and closed the door quietly behind her. Payton and Brody were sharing a private moment and she'd interrupted. If she and the American girl were going to live under the same roof, they'd have to work out some kind of signal.

Cal was waiting for her in the middle of the yard. He'd grabbed his jacket and his hat and was kicking at the dirt with the toe of his boot as she approached. "Where's your cardie?" he asked.

"I couldn't go inside. Payton and Brody were…"

Cal's eyebrow shot up. "Yeah?" He shook his head. "My little brother certainly moves fast."

"Does that run in the family?"

He forced a smile, then slipped out of his jacket and draped it around her shoulders. It was still warm from his body and Gemma pulled it tight, breathing in the scent of him. Though there were plenty of handsome men in Ireland, there weren't many who spent all day long on a horse. That kind of work did something to a man's body—made it harder, leaner…sexier.

She would find a way to kiss him tonight, to shatter his cool facade. The brief kiss they'd shared earlier had been completely one-sided. But Gemma suspected that, given the opportunity, Cal was probably a pretty decent kisser.

The way she saw it, he was likely good in bed, too. She'd heard that the quiet ones were always better. A man with an ego seldom lived up to expectations. But a bloke like Cal didn't need to prove anything. No one would ever question his masculinity. After what she'd seen in the hallway, certainly not her.

"Where are we going?" she asked.

"Walkabout," he said.

"Walkabout?"

"A stroll. It's an aboriginal term. The natives wander out into the bush and search for spiritual enlightenment. But this isn't quite so serious. I'll take you to the stables first."

"Horses?"

"That's what we keep there."

Gemma had already met the three dogs that lived on Kerry Creek. They could usually be found trailing after the jackaroos who fed and cared for them. A childhood encounter with a vicious bull terrier had left her with a healthy respect for animals in general and a long scar on her ankle. And now, she preferred to stay well clear of all of them. She couldn't control another creature's behavior and Gemma didn't like anything she couldn't control.

She lagged along behind him and when he grew impatient with her pace, Cal took her hand. "I thought we were supposed to stroll," she said.

He slowed down. "You're right. So, let me tell you about the station. We have just over fifty thousand acres, which isn't big for a cattle station. There are some outfits in Queensland with a quarter million acres. We have three thousand head of cattle and about a hundred horses. There are six full-time stockmen on Kerry Creek and next month, when we start mustering, we'll hire a few more, temporarily."

"Mustering," she said.

"We gather up the cattle into a mob and drive them into the homestead yards. We brand and tag the calves and inoculate them. Count them all up. And then ship some of the cattle to market."

"To eat," she said.

"That's where hamburgers come from," Cal replied.

"I'm aware of that," Gemma said. "But I've never really looked a hamburger in the eye while it was still alive." She turned slowly. "Where are all these cattle?"

"Out there," Cal said, pointing past the collection of buildings. "Somewhere. We have to go find them when we're ready. Teague will fly over and let us know where they are."

They stopped at a long, low building. Cal stepped inside the dimly lit interior. "Come on. There's no hamburger in here."

Gemma reluctantly followed him inside. Though the stable didn't smell like a perfume factory, she didn't find the odor completely nauseating. "The horses start foaling in the fall. We bring them into the stables after we're done with the mustering. Teague likes to keep a close eye on them."

"Don't you lose a lot of animals if you just let them wander?"

"Our land is fenced and they move in groups. There

are water tanks and troughs scattered over the station. The cattle tend to stay close to water. Most of our daily work has to do with keeping the water flowing for the stock. We spend a lot of time repairing fences, too."

"What do you do when you're not working?"

"More work. The books. Driving into town for supplies or feed. There's never really time to relax." He paused. "Come on. Let's go for a ride. I'll show you the best sights on the station." He turned and grabbed a saddle from a rack across from the stalls, hefting it over his shoulder.

"I don't ride."

"Don't worry, you can ride with me."

"No," she said, more emphatically. "I've never been on a horse. To tell the truth, they scare me."

"There's nothing to be scared of," he said with a laugh. "Come on, I'll introduce you."

Gemma shifted nervously. It was hard enough with dogs and cats, but horses were another thing. They were huge and unpredictable and smelly and they had enormous teeth. And they were probably crawling with all sorts of bugs. "Couldn't we just walk? The Irish are very good at walking."

He set his saddle down, then nodded. "Are you afraid of machines?"

"What? Like chainsaws and power drills? I'm not fond of them."

"Like motorcycles? Quad bikes?"

"Oh," Gemma said, her spirits brightening. "I like motorcycles. I have a scooter I take to work in the summer. They don't have teeth."

He blinked, then shook his head. "All right, we'll take a quad bike. But tomorrow, I'm going to teach you how to ride. You can't visit a cattle station and not get on a horse."

"Oh, I'm sure I could." She stepped back and felt her foot sink into something mushy. Gemma looked down to see that she'd walked right into a pile of horse poop. "Oh, what is this? Who left this here?"

Cal laughed. "We'll also get you a proper pair of boots. Those shoes won't last a day in the dust and mud."

"I like my shoes."

"They aren't very practical."

"I didn't buy them to be practical. I bought them because they were pretty."

He stared down at them for a long moment. "I guess they are pretty. Pretty ruined."

Gemma sent him a murderous glare. "Aren't we acting the maggot?"

"Translation?"

"You're messing with me. You think it's funny I don't like horses or horse poop or dirt or dust or lizards or spiders. I'm a woman. I'm not supposed to like those things. I'm supposed to stay clean and smell good."

He arched his eyebrow. "You can always tell me to nick off. Or tell me to get knotted. Then I'll leave you alone."

"You could help me clean off my shoe," she suggested. "Give me your hand." She held on to him for balance as she pulled the slipper off and scraped it against a bale of straw. But Cal was right. The little satin flat was ruined. Gemma hopped around to get it back on her foot without touching the dirty part. But suddenly, she lost her balance and tumbled against him.

For a long moment, he held her, his gazed locked with hers. Then, with a soft curse, Cal gathered her into his arms and kissed her. This was nothing like the kiss they'd shared over lunch. This was real and powerful, filled with desire.

Gemma's fingers clutched at the front of his shirt, holding tight for fear that her knees might collapse. The quiet, aloof man had disappeared. Cal was kissing her with a hunger that was fierce and demanding. His mouth possessed hers completely, making her thoughts spin wildly out of control.

His hands roamed over her body and Gemma lost herself in the sensations that raced through her. He held tight to her hips, pulling them against his in a provocative dance. When that wasn't enough, he slipped his hand beneath her shirt and cupped her breast, rubbing his thumb over her nipple until it grew hard.

Gemma moaned, tipping her head back as he kissed her neck. She wanted to tear off all her clothes and get naked with him, to feel his body against hers, skin on skin, flesh pressed to flesh. There was too much between them.

His jacket had fallen to the floor and Cal worked at the buttons on her blouse. As each one opened, his mouth drifted lower. But his erotic exploration ended when the sound of footsteps echoed through the quiet stable.

Gemma drew back and turned in the direction of the door. She saw Teague striding toward them in the dim interior. He stopped when he caught sight of them and Gemma quickly fumbled with the buttons of her shirt. Cal pushed her behind him, offering her the barrier of his body.

"What are you doing out here?" he asked, his voice tight, his body tense.

"I'm going for a ride." Teague pulled his saddle and blanket from the rack and hauled it toward the door on the far end of the stable. "Hey there, Gemma," he said as he passed.

"Hello, Teague," she called from behind Cal's back. He grinned at her and she gave him a wave. "Nice night for a ride."

"Can't a bloke get a minute of privacy around here?" Cal muttered. He grabbed his jacket first, then Gemma's hand. "Let's go."

When they got outside, he turned to her and slipped the jacket around her shoulders. "I'm going to warn you off Teague."

"Warn me off?"

"He can be real charming," Cal said. "But I suspect he's going to meet someone. Someone he shouldn't be meeting. Another woman."

"You think I'm interested in Teague?"

"Are you?" Cal asked.

She stared at him dumbfounded. Hadn't she made it perfectly clear which Quinn she preferred? Had Teague not come along, they'd probably be having sex right now on the floor of the stable.

"Don't answer that," he said. "It was a stupid question." He bent closer and kissed her again, softly but urgently, his lips taking possession of hers until she had no choice but to surrender. When he finally drew back, Gemma tried to think rationally.

Was she really ready to do this? Though indulging in an affair with Cal might be exciting, she'd come to Kerry Creek with a task to do. Maybe it was best to focus on that and not on the way his hands moved over her body or the way his tongue invaded her mouth when he kissed her.

"I—I should probably get back to work," she said. "And it might be better to see the rest of the station in daylight."

She couldn't read his expression in the dark. Was he disappointed? "Right," he said. "Absolutely."

They walked back to the house, her arms crossed in front of her, his hands shoved in his pockets. Now that they'd acted on this attraction, it would be difficult to go back. Already, she craved the taste of his mouth and the warmth of his body.

It was clear Cal was intent on seduction. And she was powerless to refuse him. But before it happened—if it did—she needed to think it through. There were too many traps, too many mistakes to be made. And though she intended to walk away, Gemma suspected that memories of an affair with Cal might stay with her for a very long time.

3

CAL STOOD OUTSIDE THE CLOSED DOOR of the library. He'd come in for lunch expecting to see Gemma at the table. But Mary had informed him Gemma had taken a late breakfast after sleeping in and had preferred to continue working rather than eat. Four hours later, he still hadn't seen her that day.

Things had gone balls-up at Kerry Creek. The usual balance had been completely upset by the arrival of Payton and Gemma. And Cal wasn't one to appreciate chaos.

The stockmen talked of nothing else but the two women all day long, planning ways they might charm them and even challenging each other to contests of strength to see who'd sit next to them at the dinner table. It had taken the last bit of Cal's patience to keep them focused on their work that day.

In part, his foul mood had come from a lack of sleep. Cal had spent last night wide awake, pondering the mistakes he'd made with Gemma, the last one weighing heavily on his mind. When Teague had walked into the stable, so charming and confident, Cal's jealousy had bubbled over, something he hadn't wanted Gemma to witness.

He shouldn't appear too interested and yet, he needed her to know he was attracted—wildly attracted. The kiss they'd shared in the stable was proof of that. But they wouldn't find privacy in the stable. He'd just caught Brody and Payton together, the same way Teague had caught him and Gemma the night before.

Sometimes, Kerry Creek could be a lonely place. But not anymore. Everywhere he looked there were people watching him. Except for Teague. He was off in his own world, riding out last night and returning in the early morning hours, appropriating feed from Kerry Creek to take over to Hayley Fraser at her grandfather's station, Wallaroo.

His brother apparently didn't care that the family was involved in a lawsuit with Harry Fraser, a bitter fight over disputed land on the border between the two stations. Though Teague could make his own choices, his choice to spend time with Hayley irritated Cal.

Added to that was Cal's confusion over Gemma. She obviously wasn't looking forward to seeing him again. He had spent the entire day thinking about her, working out what he'd say the next time they were together. But he'd made such a botch out of the previous evening that she preferred to starve rather than face him again.

"What are you doing lurking around out here?"

He looked over to see Mary standing in the hallway, a laundry basket clutched in her arms. "I'm not lurking," Cal said.

"What, then? Are you waiting for a bus?" She nodded at the door. "It's your library, your office. You can go in if you want."

"She's in there working."

"If she's in there, why aren't you there, too?"

"I don't want to disturb her," Cal said.

"What? Is she doing brain surgery? Designing a spaceship? All she's doing is looking at musty old books and papers, Cal. Just walk in and tell her you need to get something from your desk."

Cal shook his head. "That's too obvious," he said.

"Maybe she'd like a cup of tea. Or a biscuit. You could bring her something from the kitchen."

"That's a good idea," Cal said. "I'll get her a snack. Or make her a sandwich."

"Brilliant," Mary said. "Make enough for you both so you have a reason to sit down and talk to her."

Cal nodded. "Thanks," he said.

The housekeeper shrugged. "That's what I'm here for." She paused. "On second thought, maybe she'd like a piece of cake. Try that."

Cal strode back to the kitchen. He grabbed a knife from the drawer beside the sink and cut a huge slice of chocolate cake, then dropped it on a plate. The kettle was simmering on the stove, so he made a fresh pot of tea and grabbed a pair of cups.

He held the tray out in front of him as he slowly walked back to the library. Balancing it on one hand, Cal knocked on the door, then pushed it open. Gemma looked up from the desk as he entered.

"You don't have to knock. This is your office."

Cal swallowed hard. God, she looked even more beautiful than he'd remembered. Was it possible she'd changed in the course of a single day? Or had he forgotten how lovely she was? "The door was closed. I brought you something to eat…if you're hungry. I—I thought you might want to ask me some of those questions…." He set the tray down on the desk, then busied himself pouring her a cup of tea.

"We can do that later," Gemma said. "No hurry."

"Right." He glanced down at the leather chair and thought about sitting down. But he decided to wait for an invitation. "Well, then, I'll leave you to your—"

"Aren't you going to join me?" she asked. "There are two cups here. And one very large piece of cake." She picked up the plate and held it out to him.

Gemma poured a second cup of tea, then sat back in his leather chair. She took a slow sip, watching him over the rim of the cup. Cal met her gaze, but this time he didn't allow himself to look away. If she had any doubts about his interest in her, he wanted to dispel those immediately.

"Have you found anything interesting?"

"Your great-great-great-grandfather's diaries," she said.

"Really? Where did you find them?"

"On the top shelf, behind a stack of old ledgers. He's quite an interesting man."

"I'd heard he led an interesting life," Cal said. "But I've never read the diaries." He scooped a bite of cake onto the fork and held it out to her.

"I did some research in Dublin before I flew over here. Crevan Quinn was convicted of petty theft, but he was suspected of a much more serious crime. He was accused of stealing a valuable family heirloom by Lord

Stanton Parnell, a very powerful man." She paused to eat the cake.

"Hmm. I thought he was only a pickpocket." Cal watched as Gemma licked frosting off her lower lip, imagining that he might do the task for her. Everything she did fascinated him—from the way she held a book, to the tilt of her head when she spoke, to the way her tongue moistened her lips. It all seemed designed to intensify his desire. But how could he get from cake to kissing in one simple step?

Suddenly, he realized that he didn't have a clue. His mouth went dry and he grabbed his cup of tea. "I—I should really leave you to your work." Cal stood, his tea cup clattering in the saucer.

"No. I'm finished for—"

"I've got work to do before dinner and—"

"I'd like to chat a bit longer if—"

Cal cursed softly and she stopped speaking, her expression filled with surprise at his outburst. He closed his eyes and drew in a deep breath. Then he circled the desk and pulled her out of his chair.

This time, he didn't think before kissing her. He knew exactly what he wanted and he was prepared to make it good. When his lips met hers, she sank back against the desk, clutching at the front of his shirt. Cal held on to her waist, then slid his hands over the sweet curve of her hips.

They both reached out to push the papers and books off the desk, but a wide sweep of Cal's hand sent the tray and teapot crashing onto the thick Oriental rug. Once the desk had been cleared of everything, he picked her up and sat her on the edge, then stepped between her knees.

Her hands skimmed over his shoulders and down his chest, the sensation sending a flood of warmth through his bloodstream. He'd thought so carefully about how to handle this moment, then realized he was operating on pure instinct. He didn't need to think anymore, just feel.

He buried his face in the curve of her neck and inhaled her scent. She smelled like flowers, a pure, heady scent, nothing exotic, just fresh and clean and very feminine. Why had he never noticed this about other women he'd kissed? Was it coincidence that his senses seemed more attuned to Gemma?

Cal ran his hands over her arms, reveling in the silken feel of her skin. And when she moaned softly, her breath was warm against his ear. Time had slowed, allowing Cal to savor each moment before moving on to the next. They might have gone on forever, or the rest of the night, had they not heard the knock on the library door.

Cal stepped back, pulling her up with him until they both stood behind the desk. He quickly straightened her clothes, then strode to the door and pulled it open. When he saw Mary standing in the hall, he gave her an impatient glare.

"Sorry to disturb you, but I just wanted to let Gemma know I do laundry first thing in the morning. If she has anything she wants washed, she can bring it along to breakfast."

"Thank you, Mary," Gemma called. "And the cake was wonderful."

"Glad you enjoyed it, dear."

Cal peeked out into the hall as he closed the door. "Sticky beak," he whispered. He stepped back into the room and gave Gemma an apologetic shrug. "Mary takes very good care of us all."

"Why don't your parents live on the station?" she asked.

"They live in Sydney." He slowly crossed the room to stand next to her. Reaching out, Cal took her hand, holding it up to press his palm against hers. One by one, he wove her fingers through his. "My mum left the station when I was seventeen. She couldn't take country life anymore. Four years ago, when I took over the station, my dad joined her. He missed her, so he gave up the station to be with her."

"That's so romantic," Gemma murmured, her gaze fixed on their intertwined fingers.

"Is it?" he asked. His mother knew what she was getting into when she married his father. She was aware her life would be spent on Kerry Creek. She was the one who hadn't held up her part of the bargain. "What else do you think is romantic?"

A tiny smile curled the corners of her lips. "I think you're romantic, bringing me chocolate cake and tea…even though it is spilled all over the carpet."

"Yes, but it was worth the mess," Cal said.

"Since the cake is on the floor, maybe we should go back to what we were doing?"

"Discussing Crevan Quinn?"

"No, not that," she said. She pushed up on her toes and kissed his lower lip, then ran her tongue along the crease of his mouth. "That."

"Oh, yes," he said with a slow smile. "That was nice. Are you sure you don't want to get back to work?"

"I—I think I'm done for the day," she whispered, reaching for the buttons of her blouse.

Cal couldn't help but smile. He wasn't doing too badly. They'd gotten past their initial inhibitions and moved on to playful banter. If he trusted his instincts, he'd know what to do next. Maybe these things didn't need to be learned. Maybe they were just hard-wired into a bloke's intuition.

GEMMA BRUSHED HER HAIR out of her eyes and looked up at Callum. She sat on the desk, with Cal standing between her legs, his hands cupping her face. She felt like a teenager, caught up in a crazy infatuation with a very dangerous boy. As adults, they were perfectly capable of taking off all their clothes and shagging like bunnies, but they'd spent the last half hour kissing and touching and teasing.

Gemma ran her hand over the front of his jeans, the ridge of his erection pressing against the faded fabric. He growled softly. "See what all this pashing does to me?" he murmured.

"Pashing? Is that what they call it here?"

He nodded. "What do they call it in Ireland?"

"Shifting," she said. "And you know where that leads? To sin and illegitimate babies like me."

He stepped back. "You have a—"

"Oh, no," Gemma said. "I am an illegitimate baby myself. My mother never married my father." She paused. "I know single motherhood is pretty common these days. But Ireland is still very Catholic and my mum paid a price." It was the first bit of personal information she'd revealed. Perhaps if he understood her motives, he would accept her methods.

"Do you think that makes a difference to me?"

"No," she said, shaking her head. "I just thought you might be interested."

He fixed his eyes on hers, staring at her intently. "I am. Very interested. In you."

"So tell me a secret about yourself," Gemma urged. "Something I'd be surprised to know."

"All right. But you have to promise not to laugh." Once she nodded her agreement, he continued. "I didn't kiss a girl until I was eighteen when I lost my virginity at the local whorehouse."

Gemma gasped. "Oh, my. That is interesting."

"Don't laugh," he warned.

"I'm not. I'm just amazed. You've gotten very good at kissing since then. You're kind of like a…prodigy?"

"That is the one and only time I ever visited that place. Since then, I've found legal ways to sleep with women. Although, they did legalize the knock shops in Queensland a few years back."

"So, how was it? Did they tell you what to do?"

"I knew the basics," he said. "I had done my reading. And when you live on a station all your life, you see things. It was fine. The woman was patient and didn't laugh when I fumbled around. After it was over, I was glad because I thought I wouldn't think about sex anymore."

This time Gemma did laugh. "How'd that work out for you?"

"Not well. All I did was think about sex. All the time. After I worked my way through the single women in Bilbarra, I had to head on down the road to Brisbane. But there haven't been that many women. It's kind of hard, living in the back of nowhere."

Gemma pressed her hand against his crotch. "It is hard. Very hard."

"Stop teasing. You're touching a man who hasn't been with a woman in about six months." He nuzzled her neck. "I'm excitable."

Gemma ran her hands through his hair and kissed him again. "How did we get on this subject?"

"You wanted to know a secret. I told you one."

Though she'd love nothing more than to continue the discussion, Gemma knew exactly where it would lead. If the pashing were any measure, sex with Cal would be incredible. But she still hadn't been able to rationalize her deception. Somehow, she sensed he valued honesty far more than he needed physical gratification. He'd gone six months without sex. That took a lot of self-control.

She grabbed the front of his shirt and began to button it. "Maybe we should clean up this mess. I wouldn't want Mary to think I was a bad guest."

"I'll take care of it," he said. "This is my office, so it's usually a bit of a dog's breakfast anyway."

"And I've made it…a messy dog's breakfast?"

"A dirty carpet is a small price to pay." He tugged the front of her blouse together. "I have something to show you." He took her hand and led her to the door, but Gemma yanked him to a stop.

His shirt was half-open and she hadn't finished buttoning hers. When she'd covered everything properly, she raked her hands through her hair. "All right?" she asked.

"We're just going across the hall to the parlor," he said.

"I don't want everyone knowing what we were doing in here."

He nodded toward the clean surface of the desk. "I think they're smart enough to figure it out. We weren't polishing the furniture—or maybe we were." Cal chuckled as he opened the door. They hurried across the hall and into the parlor. He led her over to the fireplace and pointed to the portrait above it. "There he is."

Gemma looked at the painting. "Who?"

"That's Crevan. The pickpocket."

Gemma gasped. "This is Crevan Quinn?" She'd walked past the portrait several times already on her way to the front door but she'd barely noticed it. She should have asked about the painting the moment she'd seen it, but her instincts for history had been dulled by her fascination with Callum.

"That's him. It was delivered the day before he died. He had it painted in Sydney. My mum always said she was glad we got our good looks from her side of the family."

Crevan's hair was white and wild and his eyes were fierce. Gemma stepped closer to examine the canvas in detail. The coat he wore was finely tailored to his form and the background was a mix of Victorian architecture and Queensland landscape.

"He is an imposing figure," she said. Her gaze fixed on Crevan's hand. How well a subject's hands were captured was always the true mark of a great painter. He clutched an ornate walking stick with a— "Oh, my God. I can't believe it."

"I know. He was a pretty ugly bugger. But I think it's just the hair and those sideburns."

It was right there in front of her, gleaming with a green fire. She glanced over at Cal, worried that he'd noticed her reaction. In the painting the Emerald of Eire was perched on the head of Crevan's walking stick. She'd found it. Just like that, the proof had dropped into her lap. But what was she going to do with it?

"It—It's an impressive portrait," she began, trying to come up with a way to ask about the jewel. If the walking stick was still around, Cal may not even realize the value of the stone embedded in the handle.

"This is why I love history," she continued. "Look at his clothing. Do you know if he sat for this portrait or was it painted from a photograph?"

Cal shrugged. "What difference does it make?"

"Well, for instance, this walking stick. Did it belong to your grandfather, or did the painter just paint it in to make your grandfather look more prosperous than he actually was? It's a lovely stick," she added, pointing toward it. "Was it passed down in the family?"

"No, I don't think so." Cal studied the portrait more carefully—too carefully for Gemma's comfort. Had he noticed the jewel? She hadn't told him about the Emerald of Eire and for now, she was going to keep that part of her story a secret.

"There must be some family heirlooms. After all, you're living in the same house he did."

"There's a lot of stuff up in the attic," Cal said. "I've always meant to go through it and sell what we didn't need and now's as good a time as ever. Maybe you'd like to help. You'd probably know if things were antiques or just old."

"There could be family documents up there, too," she said, getting excited.

Gemma felt that wonderful thrill that came when she was on the verge of a new discovery. Usually she experienced it buried deep in a musty old archive. But here she was, standing next to a man who made her body ache with desire, faced with a choice.

A knock sounded on the door and they both turned to see Mary standing in the hall. "Did we just have a weather event I missed? It looks like a cyclone hit the library."

"I'm so sorry," Gemma said. "I'll clean it up straight off."

Mary chuckled and shook her head. "No need. Dinner is ready." She pointed to Cal's chest. "Fix your shirt. You look like an unmade bed."

After she walked away, Gemma looked up at Cal, her face warm with embarrassment. "Sorry," she murmured as she reworked the buttons on his shirt. "I guess our time together isn't a secret anymore."

"No worries. Mary is very discreet," he said.

They strolled to the back of the house, their fingers intertwined. At the last moment, he pulled her into the shadows and kissed her, long and hard, leaving her breathless. It was a promise that they'd continue what they'd started in the library.

Gemma sighed softly. It was astounding how easily

she'd forgotten about the emerald. One kiss was all it took to wipe it from her thoughts completely. David Parnell was a man she didn't even know, a fantasy father that she'd built up in her mind. But Cal Quinn was a real, flesh-and-blood male.

There was a choice to be made and Gemma was beginning to question her resolve.

DINNER THAT NIGHT WAS a rowdy affair. Teague had returned and taken his customary spot at the opposite end of the table. Brody and Payton had joined them, too, adding to the excitement. The discussion had turned to the Bachelors and Spinsters ball, a wild event held in Bilbarra at the end of the month.

Both Payton and Gemma expressed an interest in attending, but Cal had to wonder if they were serious. He couldn't imagine Gemma's work taking an entire month. Though he wasn't sure what she was looking for, there were only so many books in the library. If she couldn't find what she needed in a week or two, she wasn't much of a historian.

As for Payton, she seemed quite content to stay on at Kerry Creek indefinitely. She was doing an impressive job in the stables and was keeping Brody occupied, so Cal couldn't really complain.

Cal listened to the conversation distractedly, focused instead on Gemma's hand, which rested on his thigh, hidden by the table. No one had seemed to notice, but Cal was having a difficult time breathing.

Every now and then, she'd slowly slide her palm up and then down, coming dangerously close to his crotch.

The thought of her touching him again, the way she'd done in the library, had caused a physical reaction—his erection pressed against the denim on his jeans. He was glad that Mary had made dessert, because he wouldn't be standing up anytime soon.

"It might be fun," Payton said, her interest in the ball keen. She turned to Gemma. "What do you think? When in Australia, do as the Aussies do?"

Gemma laughed. "We'd have to get something nice to wear."

"I have dresses," Payton said. "I need work clothes. I can't wear Davey's castoffs forever. Not that I don't appreciate the loan," she said, sending the jackaroo a sweet smile.

"I have to fly to Brisbane in a few days. I could take you shopping," Teague offered.

Cal sat up, bracing his elbows on the table. "Hang on there. Gemma and Payton are not going to Bachelors and Spinsters."

"We won't participate," Gemma said. "We'll just go to…observe. Think of it as sightseeing. Or anthropological research."

"If you want to see the real sights of Australia, I'll take you," Teague said. "Queensland is beautiful from the air."

"There's an idea," Cal said. "You'd be much safer in a plane piloted by our brother than at Bachelors and Spinsters."

Gemma leaned closer to him, her hand moving up his leg again. "We could go together," she murmured, the conversation going on without them. "You are a bachelor and I am a spinster."

"It's at the end of the month," Cal said. "Are you staying that long?"

Her smile faded and she shook her head. "Probably not."

Cal watched her silently as the conversation shifted to the sights the girls ought to see in Queensland. When the meal was finished, the boys scrambled to pull out Gemma's chair, but Cal waved them off and did it himself. If his intentions regarding Gemma hadn't been made clear to the boys before this, he was making them crystal clear now. He tucked her hand in his and led her out of the kitchen toward the library, leaving behind a group of dejected would-be suitors.

Cal couldn't wait until they got behind closed doors. He pulled her into his arms the moment they were out of sight of the kitchen, his hands roving freely over her body. "You were driving me mad at dinner," he whispered, pressing her back against the wall.

"That was the point," Gemma teased.

"What am I going to do about you?" He pinned her arms to her sides. "All I ever think about is kissing you." He leaned into her. "We never finished our tour of the station. You haven't seen my bedroom yet."

"No," Gemma said, shaking her head. "It wouldn't feel right."

"I want to be alone with you." He brushed a kiss across her mouth. "Someplace where we won't be interrupted." He grabbed her hand. "I know. Come on, I'm going to show you something special."

He grabbed a jacket on their way back through the

empty kitchen and slipped it over Gemma's shoulders. Then he led her toward the machine shed. The station's quad bikes were parked outside.

"Hop on," Cal said.

"I can't drive one of these things."

"I'll do the driving."

"Aren't they dangerous?"

"I'm going to drive real slow and we're not going far. Just far enough."

Gemma hiked up her skirt and straddled the bike. Then Cal got on behind her and pushed the button on the steering yoke. The machine rumbled to life and a moment later, they were headed into the outback.

Cal knew every inch of Kerry Creek, even in the dark. The quarter moon was drifting toward the horizon, providing some light to navigate by. He leaned into Gemma as he drove, feeling the warmth of her body against his. Touching her, even in such a simple way, was almost more than Cal could handle.

After months without a woman, it was nearly impossible not to think about having sex with Gemma. He could picture it in his head, every detail of her body, they way they'd react to each other, the sensation of losing himself inside of her.

And yet, he didn't want to rush this. He wanted to take his time and enjoy the foreplay. Besides, Gemma wasn't leaving anytime soon—he'd make sure of that. He knew exactly where he wanted to take her and in the distance he saw the rock, outlined by the rising moon.

The lights from the homestead had faded in the distance and Cal turned off the bike and slid off the back. He spanned Gemma's waist with his hands and lifted her off, standing her in front of him.

"What is this?" she asked.

"The big rock," Cal explained. "It's a bit of a landmark." He took her hand and led her closer. "We always came out here as kids. The rock is supposed to have some sort of magical power. At least that's what we believed."

"How did it get here?"

"I don't know. That's a question for someone who knows about history. I think the Aborigines might have smoothed the surface and rolled it here. But they haven't claimed this as a spiritual site. It was here when Crevan bought the station. There's talk that he buried a family treasure out here."

"Really?"

"We dug for it when we were kids, turned up all this dirt around the rock, but we didn't find anything."

Gemma walked over to the massive boulder and ran her hand over the smooth surface. "Is this why you brought me to see out here in the dark?"

"Look up," he said.

She did as she was told and a tiny gasp slipped from her lips. Though the view of the stars was better once the moon set, the sky was still awash with tiny specks of light. "I've never seen so many stars in my life."

"When you live in the city, the light obscures them," Cal explained.

"When I was a girl, I used to visit my grandfather in County Clare during my summer holiday. He lived just a few miles from the ocean and he'd set up his telescope on the cliffs on a clear night and spend hours identifying stars." She turned to look at him. "Mind you, it wasn't an easy thing. A clear sky on the Irish coast can be a rare thing."

"The Quinns come from County Kerry," he said. "That's why the station is named Kerry Creek."

"County Kerry is just to the north of Clare. Who knows, our families might have been neighbors back in the day." She paused. "Have you ever visited Ireland?"

"No," Cal replied. He'd never even been out of Australia. "But I'd like to go someday. Maybe I'll come and visit you."

"Oh, you should. I could show you where your ancestors came from. There are still Quinns all over County Kerry. We could find some of your cousins."

"I'd rather spend my time with you," he said. Cal wrapped his arm around her waist and pulled her close. "I want to kiss you again."

"It seems that's all we've been doing," Gemma replied.

"If you want me to stop, I will. Just say the word."

She took a ragged breath, and for a moment, he thought she might just stop him. But then, she wrapped her arms around his neck. "I can't give you a single good reason why you shouldn't."

Cal brought his mouth down on hers, her lips parting and their tongues touching. The kiss was deep and stirring and he felt himself grow hard with desire. He pulled her hips against his, the friction sending a delicious rush of sensation racing through this body.

He'd met her on the road just yesterday morning and

here they were, lost in a passion that couldn't be controlled. They didn't feel like strangers. When he touched her, she felt as familiar as any woman he'd ever known, as if she'd been meant for him all along.

He slid his hands beneath her top, anxious to touch her warm skin. Before long, they were tugging at each other's clothes. The air was chilly, but Cal didn't notice when she pushed his shirt over his shoulders.

He leaned back against the rock and closed his eyes, reveling in the sensation of her lips on his naked chest. He furrowed his hands through her hair, moaning softly as she moved to his nipple. A flood of desire consumed his body as she traced a path across his chest.

How had he ever lived without this? Cal wondered. He'd sometimes gone months between women and barely considered it a problem. But he couldn't go a few minutes without Gemma. Every waking thought was of her, her taste, her scent and the feel of her body beneath his hands.

She bent lower, kissing his belly. He wanted to stop her, aware of how close he was to the edge. But this had turned into her seduction and he was determined to enjoy it for as long as it lasted.

When she moved to unbuckle his belt, Cal held his breath. "Be careful," he warned. She slid his zipper down slowly and he winced. He was going to make a fool of himself the moment she touched him.

Cal gently grabbed her wrist. "Wait," he said. He drew a deep breath and tried to quell his need. Maybe it had been a mistake to bring her here. This is what he'd been hoping for, wishing for, ever since he'd met her. Maybe the magic of this place was part of it.

"It's all right," she said. "I want to make it happen."

She pushed his jeans over his hips, her hands smoothing over his ass. He searched for her lips again, his kiss communicating the extent of his desire. When her fingers slipped beneath the waistband of his boxers, he was already lost in a vortex of pleasure.

Cal held back for as long as he could, determined to enjoy her touch. She stroked him slowly at first, her fingers dancing over his shaft. But when she wrapped her hand around him and increased her pace, Cal knew he was lost.

His release came fast and fierce and he groaned as he felt the spasms overtake him. The intensity of it made all attempts at control vanish and he gave himself over to the wonder of her touch.

When it was finished, he opened his eyes to find her smiling at him. "What?" he murmured.

"I guess that whole celibacy thing really doesn't work."

"I wasn't celibate by choice," Cal said. "I'm geographically celibate."

"Then I'm glad I could help out."

He grabbed her, running his hand through her hair and pulling her into another kiss. "You have no idea how grateful I am."

"I'm sure you'll be able to show me."

Cal chuckled softly. Though it wasn't the seduction he had planned, it was perfect. It had brought them to a new level of intimacy, a place where they didn't need to be afraid to show their vulnerable sides. Gemma liked him for exactly who he was. That was much more than he'd ever had with a woman before.

No matter how long she stayed or what happened between them, Cal had a feeling she was about to change his life, his outlook, maybe even his dreams. And though he had always been set in his ways, this was one time when he was ready to take a chance.

4

GEMMA SAT AT THE KITCHEN TABLE, her hands wrapped around a hot cup of tea. She took a sip, then leaned back in her chair. "How long have you worked at Kerry Creek?"

Mary set the bread bowl on the table and uncovered it, tossing the cotton dish towel aside. "Let me think. Cal was seventeen when his mother left and he's nearly thirty now. So it's coming on thirteen years." She paused. "Heavens, it seems like just yesterday that I drove up to the house with my luggage in hand."

"Did you ever want a family of your own?"

Mary punched the bread down and covered it again with the cloth, then returned the bread bowl to the top of the stove. "Of course. But the right man never came along. These days, you don't need the right man. You girls have choices."

"But we still want the fairy tale," Gemma said. "We're searching for the white knight and the castle and all the happily-ever-afters."

"And what if your knight never turns up? What then?"

An image of Callum drifted through Gemma's mind, his head thrown back, his body caught in the midst of his release. He'd rescued her once, but that wasn't the only reason for her attraction. Sometimes a girl didn't need chivalry; she needed passion and excitement. "I'm going to give him a little more time."

"Yes, I think that's a splendid idea. Give him time."

It was clear that Mary wasn't talking about a generic white knight, but about Cal. And Gemma would be thrilled to allow him all the time he needed. But sooner or later, he'd begin to wonder what she was really doing at Kerry Creek. And she'd have to explain. Then, her time would be up.

"My mother raised me alone and it wasn't easy. I have a good position at the university that pays well, but I'm not sure I'd choose to have a child on my own."

"You make do with what you have and you get by," Mary said. "She did a splendid job with you."

It felt nice to be complimented for a change. Gemma's mother had never been satisfied with anything that her daughter had accomplished. Instead, she'd been obsessed with Gemma gaining her rightful place in the Parnell family, as if that were the only route to happiness.

As she observed life here at Kerry Creek, Gemma was beginning to think that money and position weren't everything. It was the connections you made with other people that determined happiness, the people you loved and those who loved you.

"Tell me about Cal's parents. Why did his mother leave?"

Mary poured herself a cup of tea and sat down at the table. "There wasn't anything else she could do. Jack Quinn was a very stubborn man and he thought the 'for-better-or-worse' part of the vows they took was written in stone. Sarah believed marriage was a work in progress. Jack never left the station, never took a vacation. Sarah wanted to see something of the world, so she went out on her own to find it. After the boys were grown, Jack realized he couldn't do without her. Luckily, Sarah still loved him."

"Is that why Cal isn't married? Because of what his parents went through?"

"Oh, there are plenty of women who'd be happy to spend their lives on Kerry Creek. But Callum's always been a bit shy and nervous around girls."

Gemma gasped. "Cal? Shy?"

"You don't think so?"

She shook her head. "No. He's quiet and perhaps a bit aloof. A man of few words. But once he warms up, he's quite charming."

"Charming," Mary repeated. "Well, I'm glad he's finally letting someone see that side of him." She took another sip of her tea. "I shouldn't tell you this, but Cal has signed himself up for a matchmaking service. To find himself a wife."

"He told you this?"

"No. He left an advert out on his nightstand and I saw it while I was making his bed. He doesn't know I've read it."

Gemma stared at Mary, wondering why she'd chosen to reveal such news. "I would think there'd be plenty of women interested in marrying him."

"Yes. I hope so." She gave Gemma a shrewd look. "If you have any thoughts in that direction, perhaps you should speak up?"

"Me?" Gemma shook her head. "No. No, I'm not interested in marriage. Nor am I cut out for life in the outback. Believe me, I would be a disaster."

"Ah, but love can change that."

"I'm not going to fall in love with Cal," Gemma said.

"Then all this kissing and foolishness doesn't mean you're gone on him?" Mary asked.

"No. We're just having a bit of fun."

"I'm not sure he would agree," Mary said. "Take care, Gemma. Beneath that hard shell is a man who leads with his heart. You can hurt him." She drew a deep breath and smiled brightly. "So, how is your work coming along? You said you were doing this genealogy for a member of the Quinn family?"

"Yes," Gemma said. It was part of the lie, but the more she got to know the people at Kerry Creek, the more difficult it had become to deceive them.

"He must be quite wealthy to pay you to come all the way over here to do research."

"Yes," Gemma repeated. "Do you have any more of those lovely biscuits you left in the library for me?" Mary took the bait and rose from the table, returning a few moments later with a cookie tin. "These are so good. What's in them?" Gemma asked.

"Almonds," she said. "And a bit of toasted coconut. They're Cal's favorite, too."

Gemma chuckled. "Stop. We may enjoy the same biscuits, but I'm not Cal's type. Trust me."

"What makes you say that?"

"I'm terrified of animals. Dogs, horses. Insects, too. Snakes, lizards. I don't like dirt or dust. I'm a city girl…" At the sound of footsteps on the porch, she stopped.

"I see what's happening. I go to work and you two ladies spend the day sipping tea and eating bickies." Cal peered through the screen door, his hat pushed back on his head. "May I join you or is this just for girls?"

"It's just for girls," Gemma shouted in a teasing voice. "Go away."

"All right, I'll stand out here all alone, hungry and thirsty and pathetic, just a hard-working bloke with no one to pity him."

Gemma rolled her eyes, then grabbed a cookie from the tin. "Thanks for the tea, Mary. I better go see to Mr. Lonely Hearts out there."

She walked to the door and stepped out onto the porch. Callum looked around to make sure no one was watching, then grabbed her and gave her a playful kiss, pinning her up against the side of the house. "Is that bickie for me?"

Gemma stuck it in his mouth. They'd become more comfortable with each other, but there were still so many things she didn't know about him. Was he really searching for a wife? And if he was, where did she fit into the scheme?

Gemma didn't mind keeping their relationship simple. There was no need for a commitment. But she couldn't help a tiny pang of jealousy, thinking about the woman who would finally win the heart of Callum Quinn. She'd be lucky to spend the rest of her nights in his bed. "What are you doing back so soon?"

"I needed a smoko," he said.

"A what?"

"A break, from work."

"Everyday I learn something new. Bickie, smoko. Last night it was pashing. What's next?"

"I have something. Come on." He took a bite of the biscuit as he led her down the steps. His horse was tied to a rail in front of the porch and he pointed to the stirrup. "Hop on up and we'll go for a ride."

"You want me to get on that horse?"

"I'll help you. Just put your foot in the stirrup."

"No," Gemma said. "I'm not going to do that. I told you, those things frighten me."

His horse suddenly turned and Gemma jumped back and screamed. The sound caused the horse to jerk and Gemma ran back onto the porch. "See. You can never tell what they're going to do. People can get killed riding horses. I've seen it on the telly. They trip and fall down right on top of you."

"Gemma, you're being irrational. We're not going to go jumping over fences or leaping across dry creeks. We'll start with a nice, slow walk."

She crossed her arms over her chest and shook her head. Her fears might be irrational, but they were her fears and he had no right to belittle them. "No. If you need to go somewhere, go. I'm not coming with you."

He stood beside his horse, his expression unreadable. She was not going to give in on this. If he wanted a woman who could ride horses and rope cattle, then he could go find one. She wasn't going to try to make herself something she wasn't.

"I have to get back to work," she murmured, turning for the door.

He was at her side in an instant, taking the steps two at a time. "Wait." Cal grabbed her arm to stop her retreat. "What's wrong?"

"Nothing," she said, trying to maintain an indifferent expression. But it wasn't nothing. It was that same old something that always seemed to get between her and the men in her life—fear. The pattern had become so common Gemma recognized it immediately. If a man tried to get too close, she'd step away emotionally, just out of reach.

"Are you angry?"

"No."

"I think you are."

"If I brought you to Dublin and asked you to stand in front of a roomful of people and talk about Irish history, would you do it?"

"No," he said.

"Because you're not comfortable with it. I do that every day and think nothing of it. You ride your horse every day and never give the skill a second thought."

"I'm sorry," he said.

Gemma took a deep breath. "I just don't see the point. It's not like I'm going to be buying a horse and riding it around Dublin. Once I go home, I'll probably never go near one again."

"When are you going home?" Cal asked.

"I don't know. Is my welcome suddenly wearing thin?"

"No," Cal said. "I was just wondering when you had to be back. Do you have the entire summer off?"

"Classes begin in early September, but I have to be back by the middle of August to prepare."

"Good. You're welcome to stay as long as you like,"

Callum said. "I enjoy having you here. For a lot of reasons, not just the—well, you know. And I'm sorry about the horse. I was just having a bit of fun."

He was right. That's what they had together—fun—and nothing more. And she was turning it into a big drama. She'd let Mary's revelation bother her. If Cal was looking for a wife, he wouldn't find a lifelong mate in her. She was a good time, a no-strings affair, a summer holiday with great sex.

The thought caused an ache in her heart. Shouldn't she want to be someone's only love? Shouldn't she be searching for that one person who made her world complete? That's what normal, emotionally healthy people did. But Gemma knew better. That kind of commitment wasn't in her nature.

"Really, I'm not angry," she said. "And you're right. My fears are irrational."

"At least come and pet him. He's a very gentle boy. Just like me."

Gemma gave them both a suspicious look, then slowly walked down the steps. "If he bites me, I'll never forgive you."

"If he bites you, you can bite me," Cal said.

Though Gemma knew what he'd meant, it still sounded more like sexual innuendo than retribution. She stood behind him, still wary. Still, she could be a good sport about this one thing. What was the harm?

He grabbed the horse's bridle and held the animal steady. "Pet his nose. He likes that."

Hesitantly, she reached out, her hand trembling slightly. "What's his name?"

"Eddie," Cal said.

Gemma ran her hand over the horse's muzzle, then pulled it away. But Eddie wanted more and he nudged her with his nose. "It's so soft," she said, stroking him again. "Like velvet."

Whenever she stopped, Eddie found a way to get his nose beneath her hand again. Gemma giggled at his clever antics. "He's a flirt."

"Hey, don't steal my girl," Cal warned, scratching the horse behind his ears.

Gemma's heart skipped. Was that how he thought of her? His girl? "Maybe you should get Eddie a girl of his own?"

"He wouldn't know what to do with her," Cal said.

"Is he gay?"

Cal laughed, reaching out to touch her face with his gloved hand. "No. He's a gelding."

"Why would you do that to him?"

"Because all stallions think about is sex. They're very difficult to control. Geldings are much more trainable. We only have one stallion on the station and he does all the work."

"I should get back to work," Gemma said.

"Me, too." He bent close and brushed a kiss across her lips. "I'll see you later?"

"You will," Gemma said.

"I know. I like that. Knowing you'll be here when I get done with my day." He hooked his foot in the stirrup and swung up into the saddle, adjusting his hat as he twisted the reins through his fingers. "Have a nice afternoon, Miss Moynihan."

With that, he wheeled his horse around and gave him a gentle kick. Eddie broke into a brisk walk, causing dust to fly up from his hooves. Gemma watched until Callum had disappeared behind the stable, then she sat down on one of the chairs that lined the back porch.

She'd known Cal for two days and already her feelings for him overwhelmed her common sense. If she couldn't control herself, she'd have no choice but to leave. Maybe that would be best.

Gemma felt a wave of frustration wash over her. Why did it have to be so complicated? Why couldn't the owner of Kerry Creek be a grumpy old man instead of a gorgeous bloke who made her heart race and her body tremble?

THE SUN HAD GONE DOWN hours ago and night had fallen on Kerry Creek Station. Cal sat on the back porch of the homestead, staring out into the yard, a bottle of beer dangling from his hand.

Before Gemma had arrived, dawn was his favorite time of day. But now, sunset meant that his work was done and he could spend the entire evening with Gemma. Unfortunately, she seemed preoccupied with her research. She'd closed herself in the library after dinner, promising that she'd be finished soon. Now, two hours later, he was still sitting alone, his mind filled with thoughts of the time they were wasting. The sooner she got her work done, the sooner she'd leave. But he couldn't think of any way to stall her progress.

She seemed to be particularly interested in Crevan Quinn. Maybe Cal could tempt her with some inside information. He hadn't been in the attic since he was a kid, but there might be something up there worth finding. And, of course, there was the legend of the buried treasure. They could spend a year digging for that.

Family legend had it that Crevan had buried a lockbox filled with gold somewhere on the station, but he'd died before he could dig it up. The story had been passed down from generation to generation, but no one had ever found a clue as to the location. With fifty thousand acres of land, finding that box was like searching for a single grain of sand on a beach.

A movement caught his eye and Cal watched as Brody emerged from the darkness, his horse at a slow walk. Considering his little brother's dislike for station work, Cal had to wonder what he was doing riding in so late at night.

"Where were you?" he asked.

"I went for a swim with Payton," Brody replied as he dismounted. "Do you have another one of those?"

Reaching down, Cal grabbled the bottle next to his chair and held it out. "You have to go fetch the next round."

Brody flopped down next to Cal and took a long drink, draining half the bottle before he paused to belch.

"Nice," Cal said. "A bit more choke and she would have started."

"Thank you," Brody muttered. He kicked his feet up on the porch railing.

"Funny how you're on your best behavior around Payton, but when she's gone you revert back to typical Brody."

"And you don't put on airs when you're with Gemma?" Brody paused. "Why aren't you with Gemma? How come you're all alone here, crying into your beer?"

"She's shut herself in the library. I can't understand what's taking her all this time. It's not like the Quinns are royalty. But she's going over every single journal and account book in there."

"What does that have to do with our family history?"

"Don't ask me," Cal said.

"She's pretty. Not as pretty as Payton, but pretty."

Oddly enough, the insult didn't sting. He was glad Brody hadn't taken a fancy to Gemma. It left the way clear for him. Still, he had to defend her honor. "I beg to differ. Gemma is much prettier."

"Payton told me she spoke with Teague today. He was talking like he'd started things up with Hayley Fraser again. And he took off in the middle of the night last night on horseback."

Callum's suspicions had been confirmed. "Shit. When I heard she was back, I wondered if he was going to see her again. What do you think she's up to?"

"You never liked her, did you?"

That was putting it mildly. He'd been trained from an early age to distrust the Frasers. Somehow, that prejudice hadn't taken with Teague, although Cal could understand why. Hayley Fraser was a hot buttered crumpet with her blond hair and her movie-star looks. "She put Teague through hell the first time they were together. He has a blind spot when it comes to her."

"Maybe that's our problem," Brody suggested.

"We've never had a blind spot when it comes to a woman. Maybe we're missing out on something."

Cal pondered the thought as he took another swallow of his beer. "Maybe." He swung his legs off the porch railing and got to his feet. He wasn't going to miss out on anything when it came to Gemma. If he felt like being with her, then he was going to sit in the library and watch her work. "I'm going to go check on Gemma. See if she needs some help." He stepped over Brody's outstretched legs and walked back inside the house, leaving his brother alone to contemplate his own romantic inadequacies.

The kitchen was dark when he entered. The sound of the telly drifted in from the parlour. Mary was wrapped up in one of her programs, lost in the fantasy of life lived in the middle of somewhere. Was that what it took for a woman to be satisfied living in the outback? A good imagination and plenty of telly?

He thought about the three women whose profiles he'd received from OutbackMates, wondering what it was that made the outback so attractive to them. He'd been honest on his questionnaire about the amount of time he spent off the station. They knew he never took a vacation. But he had mentioned that the station had a plane. He'd thought it made Kerry Creek seem more prosperous than it was. And Teague could usually be depended upon to fly his brothers wherever they wanted to go, his work permitting.

He'd have to look at those profiles again. Once Gemma left, he'd settle back into his original plan. But Cal wondered if he'd find a woman who made him feel the way Gemma did. Did lightning strike twice? Or was it simply a matter of lowering his standards?

Cal stood outside the library door, wondering whether to knock or to just walk inside. After all, it was his office, his house, his family papers. And there was no reason why she should object. Resolved, he opened the door.

The room was a mess, books scattered across the floor, old papers littering the desk. It looked worse than it had the previous evening when they'd cleared the desk for more interesting research.

He glanced around the room, but Gemma wasn't inside. Then he heard the rustle of papers from behind the desk. Cal found her sitting on the floor, intently studying a map of some sort. "Finding anything worthwhile?"

She'd been so caught up in her work that she jumped at the sound of his voice. Gemma quickly tossed the map onto a stack of papers and smiled up at him. "No," she said. "I mean, nothing that will help with the genealogy. I—I just got caught up in all the old documents. It's the historian in me."

"No worries," Cal said. "You're welcome to look through anything in here. It's all just gathering dust anyway."

Gemma struggled to her feet, then took in the condition of the room with a startled expression. "Oh, my, I didn't mean to do this. I just—well, there's no excuse for it."

"You can leave it," he said. "Everything will be here tomorrow, exactly as you've left it."

"No, I'll tidy up."

She bent down and began to pick up the papers and books lying on the floor. Cal leaned back against the edge of the desk and watched her, his arms braced behind him. He enjoyed looking at her. She was like a beautiful sunset or a wildflower. The more you stared, the less you wanted to look away.

Every detail of her body intrigued him, from the mane of auburn hair that she casually tossed over her shoulder to the delicate fingers that picked up papers from the floor. He loved her curves, her perfect breasts, her backside, the waist he could nearly span with his hands. The thought that he could find another woman just like Gemma was ridiculous. She was one of a kind.

Cal pushed away from the desk and squatted down beside her, reaching for a mess of papers to his right. He noticed they were station accounts. "This looks boring," he said.

"It does. But look. Crevan was a meticulous book-keeper. Here, he bought a new suit of clothes for his portrait. And here's the fee he paid to have it painted. Don't you find that interesting? When he recorded this in his journal, that portrait was still just an idea. And now, over a hundred years later, it's hanging in your parlor."

Cal let the notion sink in. She was right. It was sort of interesting. He'd passed the painting nearly every day of his life and didn't think much about it. "This puts it in—"

"Context," she finished. "Do you see? Suddenly, the painting has a life of its own."

He nodded. "You really like this stuff, don't you."

"I do. It's a giant puzzle. And when all the pieces fit together, it makes the most beautiful picture. A picture into the past, something no one has seen for years and years." She paused. "But sometimes, you can't find all the pieces. That's when it's frustrating. You have to accept that things get lost over time. And what you think you might find isn't always there to discover."

Cal wasn't sure what it was, but he suddenly needed to kiss her. He slipped his hand around her nape and pulled her toward him. His lips touched hers, softly, gently. It wasn't an expression of unbridled desire, but reassurance, understanding and…

He drew back and looked down into her eyes. And affection. As much as he fought it, Cal couldn't help his feelings for her. It wasn't just about physical attraction. He truly liked Gemma. And he could come to love her.

Three days. That's all it had taken for him to fall like a stone rolled off a cliff. He was still caught in midair, dropping fast, hurtling toward— What? Would he shatter into a million pieces or would there be a soft landing below?

He pushed her back until they both tumbled to the carpet, the papers still scattered around them. His lips found hers again as he stretched out beside her. Gemma arched beneath his touch as he tugged at her blouse.

Though the kiss may have started with affection, it had quickly transformed into something entirely different. Her fingers twisted in his hair and she molded her mouth to his, challenging him to taste more deeply.

He worked at the buttons of her blouse, then moved to her jeans, then back to her blouse again. Cal wanted her naked, but he knew this wasn't the right place. When he made love to her, he wanted something more memorable than a roll on the library floor.

Unfortunately, Gemma wasn't thinking the same way. She worked at his belt until she'd managed to unbuckle it. Cal was well aware of what her touch could do to him. This time, he'd return the favor.

He grabbed her hand and pinned both her wrists above her head. A wicked smile played at her lips and she relaxed, as if she knew exactly what he had planned. He unzipped her jeans, then smoothed his hand down her belly, dipping below the denim and lace to the damp spot between her legs.

She'd made him shudder with desire and now he would do the same for her. Cal wasn't sure if it would change anything between them, but it felt right. And since Gemma had arrived, he'd learned one important lesson—to trust his instincts.

GEMMA'S BODY HAD GONE WEAK and she couldn't put a rational thought together. Instead, she surrendered to Callum's touch, a touch so intimate, so stirring, she had no choice but to relinquish control.

How had this happened so quickly? She'd been ensnared in an attraction she couldn't deny. It was so wrong, yet it felt so incredibly right. If there was an un-written code of ethics for historical researchers, she hoped there wasn't a section on taking pleasure at the hands of her research subject.

But Cal wasn't the focus of her research. He was just a bystander, a descendant of the man she'd come to investigate. What she was doing wasn't wrong. Then why did it feel that way? Was it because there was a lie hanging between them?

Cal's fingers shifted over her, his caress soft, yet purposeful. A moan slipped from her throat as she felt herself spinning toward the edge. She ought to stop this right now and confess everything. But she was afraid he'd pack up her things and send her on her way, before she'd ever know what they could have together. She didn't want him to stop.

Every touch was proof that he needed her. His kiss was restless, searching, demanding that she respond. Gemma felt completely vulnerable, as if she had no defense against his desire. She bit her bottom lip as he slipped his finger inside of her, the sensation almost too much to bear.

He took his cue from her and a heartbeat later, he began a gentle rhythm meant to drive her toward release. Gemma opened her eyes to find him staring down at her, his gaze intense. "Is this what you want?" he whispered.

"Yes," Gemma replied, a bit breathless and light-headed.

He ran his tongue along the crease of her mouth and Gemma felt the first tremors. Her body tensed and she writhed beneath Cal's hand until he found the perfect spot. And then, she was there, her body shaking in an explosion of pleasure. It seemed to go on and on, endless spasms mixed with indescribable bliss.

When it was over, he reached down to cup her cheek. "Stay with me tonight," Cal said. "I want you in my bed."

Gemma closed her eyes. She wanted nothing more than to spend the rest of the night exploring their newfound intimacy. But she was afraid of what it might mean—not to her, but to Cal. Was it just desire that drove him? Or was he looking for something more from her? She couldn't make any promises. And it was much easier to rationalize their affair when they weren't waking up together in the morning.

"Not tonight," she said. "I should go back to the bunk-house. It's getting late and you have to be up at dawn."

"I can sleep all day if I want. I'm the boss. Gemma, no one is going to say anything."

"It's not that." She reached down and fastened her jeans, then started on the buttons of her blouse. "I just don't want to get too…attached. We both know this has to end at some point and I don't want to make it more difficult."

"I don't think spending the night in my bed is going to make it any more difficult," he said softly.

There were two ways to interpret his words, Gemma thought. Either letting her go was going to be hard no matter what. Or Callum didn't plan to become emotionally invested in their affair. Oddly, both options hurt.

"You're right," he said, obviously noticing her somber mood. He got to his feet and offered her a hand. "I'll walk you back to the bunkhouse."

After he'd helped her finish dressing, Cal took her hand in his and led her through the house and out the back door. When they reached the bunkhouse, he pulled her into his embrace and kissed her.

But his kiss wasn't meant to arouse. It was full of resignation and maybe a bit of disappointment. A period at the end of a long, complicated sentence. "I'll see you tomorrow," he whispered.

Gemma stood at the bunkhouse door, watching Cal as he walked back to the house. "Well, then," she murmured. "That makes everything much clearer." A long sigh slipped from her lips and she turned and walked inside.

The interior was dark but for the light from the yard shining through the thin curtains. Payton was already asleep, curled up beneath the blankets on her bunk. Gemma flopped facedown into her bed, stifling another groan.

Gemma had enjoyed a number of serious—and sexual—relationships with men, all very unremarkable. Desire had always been stronger in the early days and then gradually faded over time until she broke it off. But what she felt for Callum was something quite extraordinary. The physical attraction between them was as palpable as an electric current racing through her body. It excited her and frightened her all at once.

She sat up and cursed softly. If there was something between them, something more than lust, she didn't want to ruin it. She needed to be honest with him, to tell him exactly why she'd come to Kerry Creek and then let the rest play out.

Gemma stood, then strode to the door. She cursed softly, then turned back to the bed. What difference did it make? It was just a small lie, nothing that would stand in the way of a physical affair.

As she walked back to her bunk, a soft knock sounded on the door. Gemma hurried across the room and opened it, peering out into the darkness. She saw Callum standing at the bottom of the steps and she slipped outside, pulling the door shut behind her. "Why did you come back?" she asked.

"I forgot to ask if you needed anything," he said. "No, that's not right. I just didn't want the night to end."

"You don't have to make silly excuses to see me or talk to me," she said.

"I wasn't—" Cal's voice trailed off. "Yeah, maybe I was. Gemma, this has all happened very quickly. It's not something I'm accustomed to."

"Nor am I," Gemma said. "It's…surprising."

"Very," he agreed. "But not unpleasant. Surprising in a good way."

"Yes. And a bit confusing."

"Are you confused? About what?"

"I came here to do a job. And I don't really like to mix my professional life with my personal one." She paused, gathering her resolve. She could tell him now. She could make him understand. "And there's something else. I—"

Gemma didn't have a chance to say any more. He took the steps two at a time, then drew her into his embrace. They came together so perfectly it took her breath away. She wanted to forget all the reasons she had refused his invitation, but she couldn't. She'd come to care about him. And with that came an overwhelming need to spare him any emotional pain. "There's something I need to tell you about my work."

"Are you working now?" he asked.

"No."

"Then we don't need to talk about it."

"But there is—"

He kissed her again, this time to silence her. How could she be faulted? She was trying to tell him, to clear up any misunderstandings before their desire was completely out of hand. But he didn't seem to care.

"Callum, I—"

"Cal," he murmured, his lips soft against hers. "No one calls me Callum except Mary. And my brothers when they think I'm acting like an arse. And my mother, when she's angry."

"Cal, I—I—" Gemma cursed inwardly. She couldn't do it. She couldn't ruin everything between them just to soothe her conscience. "I—I'm just not ready to spend the night with you. You understand, don't you?"

"Sure," he said, staring down into her eyes. "But that doesn't mean you have to go inside. We could talk. I promise, I won't ask again."

In the end, they stayed on the porch for another hour, kissing and touching, chatting softly about nothing of importance. By the time Gemma slipped back inside the bunkhouse, she was exhilarated, not exhausted.

Gemma slowly undressed, then crawled between the sheets dressed in just a T-shirt and her panties. Though Cal was a man of many contradictions, she knew he was honest and hard working, clever and self-deprecating.

He was thoughtful and a bit shy. And she knew she could trust him. He would never deliberately hurt her.

But could she say the same about herself? Whether she wanted to admit it or not, her fears about commitment had hurt a lot of men, usually when they were most vulnerable.

Tomorrow, she'd tell Cal all about the emerald. She'd explain what the emerald really meant to her relationship with her father. And then she'd be free to enjoy whatever Cal offered.

Gemma heard a rustling from the bunk on the other wall and she pushed up on her elbow and stared into the dark. "Can't sleep?"

Payton sighed deeply. "No. You can't, either?"

"No." It would be a long time before Gemma could put thoughts of Callum out of her head. She reached for the light on her headboard, then sat up, crossing her legs in front of her. "Would you care to talk?" she asked, running her hands through her hair. "I'm a good listener. All my friends tell me so."

"It's complicated," Payton replied.

Wasn't everything when it came to men? Especially the Quinns. "I can handle complicated. Is it Brody? You two seem to be…attracted."

"That's putting it mildly," Payton replied. She crawled out of bed and crossed the room, then sat down on the edge of Gemma's bunk. "Can you keep a secret?"

"Of course." Gemma had plenty of her own, so it wouldn't be difficult.

Payton lowered her voice to a whisper. "A month ago

this last Saturday, I was putting on my wedding gown in Fiji and getting ready to walk across the beach and get married."

Gemma gasped. Now that was a big secret, maybe even bigger than the secret she was keeping. "Oh, goodness. What happened?"

"I got scared and ran away." Payton frowned. "I just wasn't sure I'd found the man I wanted to spend the rest of my life with. There was just no…fire. Do you know what I mean?"

Gemma nodded. For the first time in her life, she understood how desire could burn so deep inside her that the flame never seemed to go out. "Yes," she murmured. "I know precisely what you mean."

"So I grabbed a few things and stuffed them in my bag and exchanged my honeymoon ticket for a flight to Brisbane and…disappeared into the outback."

"And here you are," Gemma said. Their stories weren't very different. They'd both landed on Kerry Creek with a boatload of baggage. Now, faced with an attraction to a Quinn brother, they were both forced to sort through it all.

Payton smiled wanely. "Yes."

"Have you called your family?"

She shook her head. "I left a message at the hotel in Fiji after I landed in Australia. I said I'd call them soon but they're going to be very angry. Not only about the embarrassment and the expense of the wedding. The gossip will be awful. I hate to even think about it now."

"What of your fiancé?"

"I can't imagine what he's thinking. I'm sure he

doesn't want anything more to do with me. Not that I want him to. I made my choice and I can live with it."

"Well, there it is, then," Gemma said, trying to put a happy face on it. "As Cal would say, no worries."

"Oh, I have plenty to worry about. Like this thing with Brody. I'm sure it's just a reaction to what I did. I was a little…repressed and now I'm testing my boundaries. The attraction will probably fade soon. But then, I'm not sure I want it to." Payton paused. "At first, I considered him just a rebound guy, but I think he might be more."

"A rebound guy?" Gemma was unfamiliar with the term, but it made a sort of sense. "I understand. But wouldn't any man who came after your fiancé be a rebound guy? So, in theory, it would be better to go out with some git after you break up so you don't waste a good bloke?"

"I suppose that would be sensible. So you think I'm wasting Brody?"

"Or perhaps, you could consider the possibility that fate has put this man in your path and the reason you ran away from your wedding is that you were really meant to be with him all along."

"No," Payton said, taken aback by Gemma's reasoning. "You think so?"

"I think it's silly to try to figure out a relationship before it's really begun. Maybe you should just let it all happen."

Payton thought about Gemma's suggestion for a long moment, then jumped to her feet. "Thank you," she said as she hurried back to her bunk. After grabbing her jacket from the bedpost, Payton headed to the door. "I'm just going to visit Brody for a few minutes. Don't wait up for me."

"I won't," Gemma called.

When the door closed behind Payton, Gemma lay back in her bunk, pulling the covers up around her chin. Good advice. Now maybe she ought to take it herself. Perhaps it was fate that had brought her here to Kerry Creek and not her search for the emerald. If she believed that, then she'd also have to believe she and Cal were meant to meet. And that whatever her motivation for coming to Australia, it didn't make a difference. It was all part of a grand, cosmic plan.

Gemma pulled her pillow up around her head and groaned. She didn't believe in fate. She'd come to Queensland for one purpose and it wasn't to fall madly in love with an Australian cattle rancher.

5

GEMMA LOOKED AT HERSELF in the small mirror above the dry sink. Though it might have served for shaving, it was impossible to judge her appearance and she wanted to look her best for this evening.

Callum had peeked in the office during lunch and told her to be ready at four. He was taking her out. Though Bilbarra was a two-hour drive, she imagined a night away from the station, away from his responsibilities and her uncertainty, might be just the thing for them both. They'd have dinner or maybe a few drinks at a pub in town.

She smoothed her hands over her dress, the prettiest choice from the small selection she'd brought along. After her shower, she'd used the last of her scented lotion to make her skin soft to the touch, suspecting he would be doing a lot of touching later. Her makeup and hair had taken an hour. And she'd even painted her toes and fingernails an enticing shade of red.

A shiver skittered though her as she thought about what might happen between them. They'd come so close over the past few days, the desire between them growing with each intimate encounter. Gemma had decided he was leaving the last move to her, allowing her to decide when they'd let passion overwhelm practicality.

"Tonight," Gemma murmured as she stared at herself. But what if he wasn't ready? He'd have to anticipate this, to have protection. He would sense this was coming, wouldn't he? If only there was a way to know for sure.

She cursed softly. Cal wasn't an idiot. And if he forgot the condoms, then he'd have to suffer the consequences. Gemma smiled. Besides, there were other things they could do that didn't involve full-on, toe-curling, mind-blowing sex.

A knock sounded on the door and she took a deep breath and hurried across the room to answer it. Cal stood on the other side, his hair damp from a shower. But he was still dressed in work clothes.

"Aren't you ready?" He frowned. "You're not planning to wear that, are you?"

Gemma glanced down at the dress. "Not nice enough? Where are we going?"

He sighed, then took her hand. "It will do. Come on, we have to leave now if we're going to get there in time."

His ute was parked in front of the bunkhouse, the engine running. Cal helped her inside and then jogged around to the driver's side. He hopped in, then reached over her and grabbed the seat belt. "You're going to need this," he said.

He threw the truck into gear, then drove out of the yard, in the opposite direction of the road. Before long, the truck was on rough terrain and Gemma was forced to hold tight to the grip above the window. They bounced over uneven ground, at times so bad that she felt as if she were on a carnival ride.

"Is this a short cut?" she asked. "Isn't Bilbarra the other direction?"

"Who said we were going to Bilbarra?" He glanced over at her. "Did you want to go to Bilbarra?"

"You said we were going out. I thought—"

"We are going out. This is out in the outback. Bilbarra is in."

"I see I've run right up against the language barrier again," she said. "And we both speak the same language."

"What were you hoping for? Drinks? Dinner? Dancing?"

"Maybe," she said.

"There'll be all of that," Cal said with a grin. "Be patient."

"Is there a nightclub out here that no one knows about?" Gemma asked.

"Yes," he said. "It's very exclusive. We'll be lucky to get in. Especially the way you're dressed."

Gemma couldn't help but laugh. Cal was usually so serious around her, so intense. But tonight he was different—relaxed and happy, as if he were anticipating a good night. He'd even managed to tease her, something he hadn't done in the past. "What has put you in such a good mood?"

He turned to her and smiled. But just as he did, the ute hit a deep rut and Gemma slammed against the door. She cried out as her shoulder throbbed with pain. Quickly, Cal pulled the truck to a stop.

"Christ, I'm sorry. I wasn't watching. Are you all right?"

"Fine," Gemma said, rubbing her arm. "It's going to be ugly in a few days, though." She looked up at him. "I bruise very easily. First it's purple, then green, then yellow. A rainbow of ugly."

Cal took her arm and examined it, his hands smoothing over her skin. "There?" he asked.

Gemma winced as she twisted in her seat. "Yes."

He bent close, slipping his fingers beneath the loose sleeve of her dress, before pressing his lips to her shoulder. "Better?"

She held her breath and he turned to her. His lips were so close and yet he hadn't made a move to kiss her. Gemma waited. "Not quite," she murmured. "Try again."

He tugged at her dress, pulling it down to expose the curve of her neck. "Here?" he asked.

"No."

Cal moved to the base of her throat. "Then here."

Gemma moaned softly. He was seducing her. Finally. And she wasn't going to stop him. They wouldn't be interrupted this time. There'd be no knock on the door or problem that needed to be solved. She reached for the buttons of her dress and unfastened the top one.

Cal drew away and reached for the next button. But to Gemma's surprise, he fastened the first. "We still have a ways to go," he said. "Are you good?"

"Yes, I'm fine," Gemma sputtered. Either he wasn't

really interested in seducing her or he had supernatural self-control. She slid across the seat and buckled her seat belt again.

He put the truck in gear. "Don't worry," he murmured. "It will be worth the wait."

Gemma wasn't sure whether he was talking about the destination or the sex. She hoped it was the latter because it was becoming nearly impossible to think of anything else. But her excitement was slightly deflated by the knowledge that she still hadn't told him about her secret. And the longer she kept it, the more difficult it would be.

Though she'd worked hard at her research over the past few days, it didn't seem to mean as much as it had back in Ireland. At home, she could think of nothing but carving out a spot for herself in her father's life, certain it would be the answer to all of her doubts. Not to mention the answer to her mother's prayers.

She'd gone through enough self-help books to recognize that her issues with both her parents had spilled over into her own life. By trying to replace her absent father, she'd found herself attracted to older men, and men who were...unavailable. Growing up with a distant mother had left Gemma with a sense of fear and an inability to commit.

Her relationship with Cal was already doomed. He lived in the middle of nowhere, on a continent half a world away from Dublin. He was looking for a woman who could help him run the station, not some silly Irish girl who was frightened of horses and hated getting dirty. Her idea of a night out included civilization, maybe a linen tablecloth and a decent glass of wine. His included bouncing around the countryside looking for God-knows-what.

The sun was beginning to go down and Gemma wondered if they'd ever find the road. Cal pulled the truck to a stop, then jumped out. He opened her door and waited. "We're here?" Gemma asked, looking around. This spot didn't seem any different than the landscape they'd passed along the way.

"We're here," he said.

Gemma stepped out of the truck. He took her hand and tucked it into the crook of his arm, then started toward a clump of trees. As they came closer, she noticed tiny glimmering lights shining through the leaves. A moment later, she saw a canvas tent and a small table set up in front of it. "Oh," she murmured as they stepped into the small bower. "It's lovely."

Cal had strung lanterns in the trees, the light wavering in the soft breeze. The camp was set beside a small pool of water, hidden from outside view. "Did you do this?" she asked.

Cal shook his head. "That tree fell over the creek and during the rainy season, all that debris piled up making a dam. The water gathers in that low spot and—"

"I meant the camp," Gemma said.

"Yes," he said. "I found this spot a few years ago. No one knows it's here. Except maybe a few thousand head of cattle. But they're not here right now." He grabbed her hand and pulled her toward the table. "I brought wine. And Mary made us dinner. In about an hour, there will be a spectacular sunset."

"And to think I was expecting a silly restaurant."

"Would that have been better?" Cal asked.

"No," she said. "This is perfect." And it was. He'd taken the time to bring all these things out into the bush, getting each lamp in place ready to light and setting the table. She walked over to the tent and peeked inside. The canvas floor was covered with a rug and he'd arranged pillows on top of an open sleeping bag. "When did you do this?"

"This morning. I figured we needed to get away. The stables are Brody's territory and the old shack is where Teague is meeting Hayley. We needed a spot of our own." He walked to the table and poured a glass of wine for her, then held it out. "It's Australian."

"Thank you," Gemma said. He poured another glass for himself, then grabbed the bottle and led her down to the small pond. They sat down on a fallen tree, staring toward the western sky as the sun sank closer to the horizon. "This land is so different from Ireland," she said. "There, everything is green. Here, everything is…"

"Ochre," he said. He bent down and ran his finger through a small spot of mud. Then he reached out for her face. Gemma drew back, but Cal smiled. "Don't worry. It's just mud."

He smeared a bit on each cheek, then did the same on his own face. "Now, you're part of it," he said. "And this land is part of you."

"What does that mean?"

"You can't leave this place. And it will never leave you."

Gemma wasn't sure about the sentiment. They both

knew her home was in Ireland. Was he really hoping she'd decide to stay? This was turning into something far more serious than she'd ever wanted. She was caught between romance and reality. Gemma had assumed that if she ever fell in love, all her choices would be simple. But with Cal, her feelings became more complicated with each passing day.

Though Gemma knew he deserved the truth about her motives, she realized that telling him would do more harm than good. Why hurt him? Why risk the chance that he'd send her away? If she found the emerald, then she'd explain herself and hope for the best. But until then, why borrow trouble?

And if there came a time when she wanted him more than her place in the Parnell family, then she should be willing to give up her search for the emerald altogether. It was just a silly jewel, an object that was no more special than the rock sitting by the edge of the pond.

"What is it?" Cal asked. "You're staring at that rock like it's about to move."

Startled out of her thoughts, she glanced up at him. "I'm fine."

"You looked troubled." He paused. "Gemma, nothing is going to happen here unless you want it to."

"I do," she said. "I want you. I have since the day you changed my tire on the road."

He brought his hands to her face, smoothing his thumbs over her mouth. Then he leaned forward and kissed her, his lips lingering over hers, tasting and then retreating and then tasting again. Gemma slipped her arms around his neck and pulled him closer, this time kissing him with a fierce urgency. They'd waited long enough.

CAL DEEPENED THE KISS, tangling his fingers in her hair as he molded her mouth to his. He thought it might be too soon, that he was rushing things. But Gemma was pliant and willing in his arms, her lips communicating her need.

He'd been thinking about this moment ever since he'd set eyes on her, yet Cal hadn't allowed himself the luxury of believing it might come to pass. But this place provided perfect isolation with nothing to distract them but each other.

The sky in the west had turned into a kaleidoscope of colors—pink and orange and violet. He'd brought her here to enjoy the sunset, but beautiful sunsets were a commonplace in the Queensland outback. Beautiful women weren't, at least not on Kerry Creek.

As he slowly undressed her, Cal took in the details of her body, all the small characteristics that he wanted to remember. Her skin was like silk beneath his calloused hands, her flesh warm and supple. When he'd finished with the last button on the front of her dress, Cal pushed it off her shoulders and it dropped to the ground.

She wore lacy underwear, a matching set, in a pale blue that he found much sexier than black. She looked as fresh as a spring flower, so sweet and natural. He'd only imagined what she might look like naked, but now his fantasies were confirmed. She had a body any man would worship, with the delicate limbs and graceful curves of a Greek goddess.

Cal drew his hand over her shoulder and down her arm, reminding himself not to rush. He might have just one night with her and he wanted to make it memorable. When she went home to Dublin, he needed to know she'd be lying alone in bed, thinking of what they'd shared.

The wind rustled in the leaves above their heads and Cal watched as Gemma carefully unbuttoned his shirt. Once she'd pushed it aside, her lips found a spot in the center of his chest and she kissed him there. He smoothed her hair back from her face as she moved to his nipple, gently teasing it until he moaned.

Satisfied, Gemma moved to the other side, slowly exploring along the way. Waves of pleasure washed over him, but it was sweet torture and he had to stop himself from taking control, from satisfying the desire that raced through his body like a wildfire.

Her fingers fumbled with the button on his jeans and Cal stepped back. Bending over, he tugged off his boots and tossed them aside, then pulled off his socks. His jeans were next and Cal skimmed them over his hips and stepped out of them, leaving him in only his boxers.

Gemma smiled, her hands dancing over his chest. "Now what?"

"Just one thing," he said. Cal took her hand and pulled her along to the water's edge. He reached down and dunked his hand in the coolness, then gently cleaned the mud off her face. "Dirt doesn't taste very good."

"Are you planning to lick my face?" Gemma asked.

"I don't know. I kind of want to leave my options open."

She wet her hands and returned the favor. "Me, too." Gemma glanced down at her toes, then winced. "Wait, I just want to rinse off my feet."

Cal laughed. He knew her dislike of dust and dirt. "Go ahead, wade in."

With mincing steps, she walked through the shallows at the edge of the creek, but the bottom was muddier than the bank and she turned back to him, frowning.

Cal walked to her and wrapped his arms around her waist. "Okay, wash them off."

Gemma fluttered her feet in the water. When her feet were clean, Cal boosted her up until he was carrying her in his arms. Her eyes went wide and she laughed and he walked away from the creek. He finally put her down inside the canvas tent, the rug soft beneath her damp feet.

"Happy?" he asked.

Wrapping her arms around his neck, she pushed up on her toes and kissed him again. "I think I am."

Her body was made for his touch. Her breath came in quick gasps as he cupped the soft flesh of her breast. Everything about this was different. He wasn't interested in just the physical sensation of sex. Cal wanted more, a way inside her heart, a way to reach her soul. He drew her down onto the rug, grateful that he'd thought to make the tent more comfortable.

"You're the most beautiful thing I've ever seen," he whispered as he stretched out beside her.

Gemma turned to face him, her hand draped over his hip. "I'm glad you brought me here."

"I've always come here alone. It's going to be difficult not to think of you here now."

"Maybe we shouldn't—"

He pressed his finger to her lips. Cal wasn't sure what this all meant and maybe he didn't really care. He wasn't worried about a boyfriend back home. He didn't want to hear why a relationship with Cal wouldn't work. None of it made a difference. "I just want these next few hours with you. Maybe the entire night. That will be enough."

She ran her fingers through his hair. "All right."

It was an understanding, Cal thought. If they didn't complicate matters, then maybe what they shared wouldn't turn bad in the end. He could let her go, watch her walk away, as long as he felt they hadn't held anything back while they were together.

Cal took her by the waist and pulled her on top of him. She wriggled, her hips moving against his, creating a delicious friction. He was already hard and ready, but in no hurry. Sliding his hands from her backside to her bra, he unhooked it as they kissed.

Without breaking contact, Gemma discarded it, then pushed up to straddle his waist. Her hair fell over her shoulders and brushed against her face. Cal wound a strand around his finger and tugged her closer. Then he sat up and buried his face against her soft breasts.

Everything he'd wanted was here. Though fate had brought them together, he had to believe it was for more than just one night. His lips found her nipple and he teased it to a peak with his tongue. The smell of her skin was like an aphrodisiac, making him dizzy with desire.

The seduction was slow and deliberate, Cal taking his

time with each inch of naked skin. He rolled her beneath him, drawing her leg up along his hip. Gemma's eyes were closed and a tiny smile curled the corners of her mouth.

He kissed a trail to her belly, then twisted his fingers through the lacy scrap of her panties. An instant later, they were gone and he found the damp spot between her legs. Gemma cried out as he began to caress her with his tongue. Her response was so sudden that at first, he thought she wanted him to stop. But then, her fingers grasped his hair, a silent invitation to go further.

Her body was his to command and he brought her close, then rescued her from the edge. Each time, she became more desperate for release and each time, he wouldn't allow it. He wanted to share it with her, to be buried deep inside of her when she finally let go.

She was ready, but Cal wasn't sure he was. Just the thought of losing himself inside of her was enough to make him come. Could he even maintain a shred of self-control, or would she drive him to the end in just a few seconds?

He rolled away from her to retrieve the condoms he'd brought along and when he returned, she was watching him. Gemma held out her hand and he placed the box in her palm. She knelt in front of him, her fingers wrapped around his shaft, her eyes glazed with passion.

Cal held his breath, her touch nearly overwhelming him. He grabbed her wrist to slow her pace and she stopped, then pushed him onto his back. He closed his eyes as she sheathed him, grateful that the barrier between them might give him more time.

Once again, she straddled him, bracing her hands on his chest as she moved above him. And then, he was inside her, her heat surrounding him. Cal grabbed her hips. "Wait," he whispered.

"I can't," she said. "Don't make me."

He loosened his grip and she began a slow, careful rhythm, rocking forward on her knees, then back until he was buried deep. Cal had never felt such exquisite pleasure before. He'd never wanted to completely possess a woman, but was instead happy to take his pleasure without any promises.

But as he drove into her, Cal realized that this was exactly what he'd sought all along, this woman with the wild auburn hair and the porcelain skin. Everything about her fascinated him and though he'd convinced himself that one night with her would be enough, he now knew that a thousands nights wouldn't come close to satisfying him.

He felt her tense and Cal opened his eyes to see Gemma dissolve into a shattering orgasm, her fingers digging into his chest and her head thrown back. It was all he could take and a moment later, Cal thrust hard and let himself surrender.

The spasms seemed to go on forever, both of them caught up in the pleasure. When she finally collapsed onto his chest, Cal was spent, his breath coming in deep gasps and his heart slamming inside his chest.

Though they might not have scored many points for stamina, the intensity had been more than enough to banish every other sexual experience from his memory. From now on, Gemma would be the standard by which all other women were judged.

Her teeth chattered and Cal hugged her tight. "Are you cold?"

"No," she said softly. "Yes, maybe."

He gently rolled her to her side, then reached out for the down sleeping bag that he'd brought along. Wrapping it around her naked body, he pulled her back into his embrace. "Better?"

"Yes." She smoothed her fingers over his still-hard shaft, sliding the condom off and tossing it aside.

"Is there anything else you want?" he asked. Her hand tightened and he groaned. "Besides that?"

Gemma bent her arm and cupped her chin in her palm, observing him through sleepy eyes. "I'm famished."

"So sex makes you hungry?"

"Ravenous," she said. "The better the sex, the more I eat."

"So, how hungry are you? A snack or an entire meal?"

"Are you asking how it was?"

Cal nodded.

"Seven-course meal. With dessert. And in case you're interested, no man has ever gone past a burger and a bag of crisps."

"A seven-course meal. This I'd like to see."

Gemma giggled. "I might embarrass myself, so be warned. And don't get between me and chocolate, because you'll be risking grave bodily injury."

"I'll be right back," he said. "Don't go anywhere, all right." He dropped a kiss on her lips, then crawled out of the tent. The sun was about to set and the sky was ablaze with color. It was a perfect evening, the air cool and the breeze clean.

Cal stretched his arms over his head, then drew a deep breath. This was why he loved the outback. Every day brought surprising changes.

GEMMA SAT IN THE CENTER of the spacious tent, Cal's sleeping bag wrapped around her naked body. Their dinner was spread out in front of her. She picked at a piece of baked chicken with her fingers. "Didn't I warn you?" she asked, holding out a morsel for Cal.

He leaned over and she placed it in his mouth. But he grabbed her hand and slowly sucked on the tip of each finger. "You did. But I wouldn't have believed it. What else don't I know about you?"

The question caused an unusual silence and she nervously began to rearrange the items on the rug in front of her. "I have many secrets," she said.

"Tell me just one."

"I'm the daughter of a British lord. A peer of the realm."

"You're royalty?" Cal asked.

"Nobility. Illegitimate nobility," she added. "That's the important qualifier. My father doesn't recognize me as his own."

"Couldn't you get one of those tests, the DNA thing?"

"My mother insisted she didn't need one. She knew for sure. I think it was because she still loved him and hoped he'd come back to her someday. She didn't want to make him angry." Gemma laughed in amazement. "Can you imagine that? It's been twenty-eight years since he walked out of her life and she's still waiting for him to return."

"Love can make people do strange things," Cal said.

She shrugged. "He has another family. Kids and a younger wife. She's only ten years older than me."

"So you see him?"

"Oh, no. Just a time or two. He gave me money for university and that was it. I guess that's more than I should have expected. Sometimes I wonder if love is made to last a lifetime. What do you think?"

"Don't ask me. My mother left the station when I was seventeen."

"That must have been hard," she said.

"Station life was hard. My father can be pretty stubborn and he never wanted to take time away. He didn't trust anyone else to manage the day-to-day business. She decided she wanted something more out of life than the drudgery and isolation."

"I'm sorry," she said.

"Don't be. They're back together and living in Sydney. My father decided she was more important to him than the station."

"And what would you do if you fell in love with someone who didn't want to live here?"

"I wouldn't fall in love with that person."

"Sometimes you can't help who you love."

"And sometimes you can," Cal said.

Gemma recognized the truth in his words. She'd spent her whole life avoiding love, trying to convince herself she could live without it. But here, with Cal, she wanted to believe it was possible. Maybe two people could find each other in this big, lonely world.

"Are you finished?" he asked, pointing to the food.

Gemma nodded. "Why, did you bring more?"

Cal laughed. "I do like a woman who enjoys a good meal."

"I do. Especially when it's made by someone else. I'm a horrible cook."

"But can you dance?" he asked. "I promised you drinks, dinner and dancing." Cal held out his hand. "I don't really dance, but I'm willing to give it a try."

"Now? We're naked."

"That will make things much more interesting." He stood, then helped her to her feet before leading her out of the tent. The lanterns still glowed from the trees, casting a soft light around the camp. He left her standing in the middle of the glade and then returned a moment later with a portable CD player.

A moment later, a soft, slow ballad drifted into the cool night air. Cal pulled the sleeping bag around them both and began to move to the music. Gemma had danced with men before, but never had it been so strangely erotic. She felt like a pagan, caught in the midst of a strange sexual rite. All of the fears and insecurities she used to have were falling away, leaving her to act on pure emotion.

His body was strong and hard against hers, their movement generating its own warmth. Gemma grabbed the sleeping bag and tossed it aside, leaving them both naked. She tipped her head back and drew a deep breath, then slowly let it go.

This was her life, this moment in time, with this man in her arms. Nothing else mattered. She'd discovered the passion that had always been lacking before and Gemma wanted to push the boundaries, to see how much more was possible.

She let her hands trail over his body as she danced, creating a provocative counterpoint to the music. Then she stepped back and continued moving, her body relaxed and sinuous. The light from the fire flickered on her skin and she imagined herself in an old pagan fertility rite, meant to lure a man into the dark world of uncontrolled desire.

Gemma felt his eyes on her body almost as if he were touching her. She ran her hands along her torso and down to her hips, then back again. Her actions instigated a moan from the other side of the fire. And when she returned to him, he was completely aroused.

Drawing her fingers over his hard shaft, she danced around him, circling, her breasts brushing against his back, her hands searching for another spot to caress. Cal kept trying to touch her, but she evaded his embrace, preferring to continue the teasing seduction.

"Are you trying to drive me mad?" he asked, yanking her against his body. "Because it's working."

"Remember this," Gemma said. "Remember how much you want me." She reached up and smoothed her hand over his eyes until he closed them. "There." She slowly stroked his shaft. "Remember how this feels."

"I don't think I could forget even if I wanted to," Cal said.

If she found the emerald, then she'd tell him the truth. And when she did, she'd bring him back to this moment, to prove that it really made no difference at all. But until the emerald was in her possession, she wouldn't allow herself any guilt over what they shared.

She realized now that she needed a lover much more than she needed a father. The past was history and nothing could be done about it. But she lived in the present. And in the present, there was only one man in her life and he was standing naked in front of her.

6

CAL HEARD THE PLANE FLY OVER shortly before dusk. He walked out of the stables and stared up into the late afternoon sky, watching as Teague circled to land.

He'd spent the day trying to stay occupied with work, but lately it had become impossible to go an entire eight hours without taking a break or two to drop in on Gemma. Yesterday, he'd come in for midmorning tea, stayed for lunch and then returned two hours early for dinner.

He'd joined Gemma in the library, working on his station accounts as she pored over stacks of old papers. He ought to feel thankful that his ancestors had maintained such meticulous records. It was the only thing keeping her on Kerry Creek.

Though they weren't always touching, it was satisfying just to be in the same room with her. He found endless pleasure in observing her, taking in the tiny details of her behavior—the way she held her pen, the single lock of hair that she constantly tucked behind her ear, the soft sigh that slipped from her lips when she put down a book or paper.

Since their evening in the outback the night before last, their relationship had changed. Cal smiled. No, it hadn't changed. It had simply begun. Now, they both acknowledged a connection, an attraction that neither one of them wanted to deny. He could touch her at will and she responded without hesitation.

Work had been pushed aside for play, and the library door locked against interruption. Yet, there was still something standing between them. The end of all this passion and desire. It hung over them like a dark cloud, a ceaseless reminder that they were just enjoying a stolen holiday from the real world.

The more he thought about it, Cal had to wonder if Gemma had a man waiting for her in Ireland. It was impossible to believe that a woman so beautiful was all alone, that her bed was empty and her desires unfulfilled.

Cal jogged down the steps and walked to his ute parked nearby. He jumped behind the wheel and before long, was turning the truck toward the landing strip. By the time he got there, the plane had already touched down and had come to a stop at the end of the dirt runway.

Tugging his hat down against the dust cloud from the propeller, Cal opened the passenger door as Teague shut down the single engine. Payton smiled at him, handing him a cluster of shopping bags as she nimbly jumped down to the ground. Cal set them at her feet, then turned to help Gemma out.

Unable to resist and seeing no reason to hide his feelings from Teague or Payton, Cal set Gemma in front of him, then gave her a quick kiss. "Welcome back," he murmured, a smile twitching at the corners of his mouth.

A pretty blush stained Gemma's cheeks as she glanced around. "Thanks."

Cal helped Teague tie the plane down, then walked with them to his ute. He saw Payton's disappointed expression as he opened the door of the vehicle and pulled the seat forward so she could climb in the back. "He took off about a half hour ago. On horseback, toward the west. I'm sure he'll be back soon."

When they got back to the homestead, Payton headed for the stables, determined to ride out to meet Brody. Teague disappeared inside the house, whispering to Cal that he needed a beer after spending so much time inside a small plane with two chatty sheilas. That left Gemma standing alone next to the ute.

He grabbed her bags. "Did you have a nice time?"

She nodded. "Payton is a lot of fun. We laughed and talked. She's a bit crazy. And we drove Teague mad, I'm sure. Had there been a parachute handy in the plane, he might have been tempted to jump out."

"What's the deal with Payton?" Cal asked, steering her toward the bunkhouse. "What's going on between her and Brody?"

"What do you mean?"

"Brody met her in jail. I'm not certain he knows anything about her, except that she's American."

"Don't worry. She's not a criminal, if that's what you're thinking." Gemma paused as they reached the steps of the bunkhouse. "We all keep a few secrets. Even you."

Cal feigned surprise. "Me? I don't have any secrets. You tell me a secret I'm keeping and I'll tell you if you're right."

She opened the door to the bunkhouse and stepped inside. "If I knew a secret about you, it wouldn't be a secret anymore, would it?" Gemma reached for one of the bags, dogging around inside. "I bought you something."

"Yeah? Something nice that you can wear and I can remove?"

She pulled a shirt from the bag. "I saw this and thought of you. Blue is your color." Holding it out in front of him, she gave it a critical eye. "Teague tried it on for me. He said you wear the same size shirt."

"It's nice," Cal said, fingering the fabric. Not what he was hoping for, but then sexy underwear wasn't the most practical gift. "But it won't hold up for work."

"It's not for work. It's for…"

"For what?"

"For dressing up. For going on a date."

"Are we going on a date?"

"No. It's for after I leave."

Cal gave her a shrewd look. Where was this conversation headed? "Am I going on a date I don't know about?"

Her gaze met his. "Mary told me about the matchmaking service," she admitted. "I know you're looking for a wife, Cal. And I just thought I might be able to give you a few pointers."

Her words caught him completely off guard. But as he considered the revelation, her reticence suddenly made sense. She'd been afraid to become too attached, knowing that the day she left Kerry Creek, he'd start the search for a lifelong mate. "No," he said. "Mary has it wrong. She saw something she shouldn't have and made a mistake. That's what comes from being a sticky beak."

"It's not true?"

"It was something I'd considered…briefly. Until you came along."

"And now you're not considering it anymore?" Gemma asked.

"Not at the moment."

"I can't stay here, Cal," Gemma said. "You understand that, don't you? I have a career in Dublin. I can't be your wife."

"Sure," Cal said, trying to appear indifferent. "Of course, I know that. I'm not asking you to stay. I just thought as long as you're here, we'd enjoy our time together. No strings. I've got plenty of time to think about the future."

"Good," Gemma said, nodding her head. "I'm glad we have that worked out."

But it wasn't worked out, Cal sensed. For some reason, she seemed quite unsettled by the subject. "A lot of fellas do it," he said. "Living in the outback, it isn't easy to meet people. And there are practical reasons for a matchmaking service."

"But, how will you know? I mean, are you willing to settle for a woman who doesn't make you…wild with desire?"

"I'm willing to admit that companionship can sometimes be more important than incredible sex. And I'm hoping for the best."

She drew a sharp breath, then nodded. "Well, dressing a bit nicer would help. What do you think of the shirt? Try it on."

"I'll try it on later," he said. This didn't feel right. He

didn't want to think about any other woman but Gemma. He didn't want to believe she'd ever leave. Sure, he was living in a fantasy world, but why not? Why couldn't he have this for as long as it lasted? When it was over, he'd find a way to get on with his life, but not until then.

She reached up and began to unbutton his shirt. "I want to see what you look like wearing it."

"Why?" Cal asked. "What difference does it make?" When his shirt was open to the waist, he hooked his finger beneath her chin and turned her gaze back to his. His lips covered hers in a long, slow kiss, perfectly calculated to make Gemma forget everything but the desire they shared.

She sighed softly, the gift forgotten as it dropped to the floor. Gemma's arms wrapped around his neck as she surrendered to the kiss. Every sensation that washed over him was pure perfection and Cal enjoyed the feel of her body beneath his hands. Why couldn't he have Gemma? Why couldn't she be the one for him? Fate had thrown them together, but it had also played a cruel trick, waiting in the shadows to snatch her away again the moment he realized he couldn't live without her.

His fingers twisted in the hem of her shirt and in one smooth motion, he pulled it over her head, barely breaking the contact between their mouths. His hand cupped the warm flesh of her breast, her nipple hard beneath the lacy bra. This was what he loved about Gemma, the softness, the sweetness that he'd never found in any other woman.

When he touched her, he felt like a man who might

be able to love, a man who might live for just one special woman. But Cal sensed that what was special about Gemma had more to do with his ever-growing feelings for her than the scarcity of women in his life.

Her fingers worked at his belt and when she'd unfastened it, she began with the button and zipper on his jeans. He held his breath as her fingers brushed against his crotch, his cock already hard and aching for release. Her hand slipped beneath the waistband of his boxers and the moment she touched him, Cal forgot all his doubts.

If he focused on the present, on the way she stroked him, then he wouldn't have to worry about the future. He could store this all away in his head, every caress, every wild sensation, so that he might recall it later, when Gemma was gone.

Cal pulled her back toward the door, then reached around and locked it. Though Payton had gone out to find Brody, he wanted to make sure they weren't interrupted. Slowly, he stripped off her clothes, item by item, tossing them aside until she was completely naked.

Her body was made for his touch. Every part of her was exactly what he needed to light his passion and to stoke his desire. "I want you," he murmured, his mouth pressed to her throat. "Only you."

Gemma tipped her head back as his fingers tangled in her hair. Another moan tore from her throat as his other hand moved to the damp spot between her legs. He was desperate to be inside of her, to feel again that sense of connection that had faded during their day apart.

It was difficult to comprehend the depth of his need. It pulsed from every cell in his body, an undeniable force that made wanting her almost painful. Was he that weak that he couldn't resist her? Or had he already given up trying?

Cal kicked off his boots, then stripped off the rest of his clothes. The bunkhouse was nearly silent. The sound of their breathing was all that could be heard, quick gasps and gentle sighs, each a reaction, a plea, an invitation.

Though it wasn't the most romantic place to make love, Cal knew he'd never step inside the south bunkhouse again without remembering what her body looked like in the dwindling light filtering through the dusty windows.

"You're the only one," he whispered as he pinned her against the wall, his fingers laced with hers. Drawing her hands over her head, he kissed her again. "You're the only one I've ever wanted."

"No," Gemma murmured.

"Yes," Cal said. "At least, give me that. Don't make me deny what I feel."

He drew her thigh up along his hip, causing his shaft to rub slowly against her sex. This was paradise right here, with Gemma. And he'd enjoy it while it lasted.

GEMMA LEANED AGAINST the stable yard fence, her arms folded over the top rail, her chin resting on her hands. The three Quinn brothers were sitting on their horses at the far side, deep in discussion. Every now and then, they looked over at the trio of women, as if trying to guess what she, Payton and Hayley Fraser were talking about.

"I know how Brody and Cal feel about me," Hayley said. "And I don't think they were too chuffed to see me turn up here."

Gemma had been living on the station for exactly a week and in honor of the Queen's birthday, Cal had decided to arrange an impromptu celebration. The camp-drafting competition had already begun among the jackaroos when Teague had arrived with Hayley in tow.

She was a stunning beauty and according to Payton, a famous television star in Australia.

"Whatever is going on in their heads has nothing to do with us," Gemma said.

"Sistahs before mistahs." Hayley and Gemma both turned to stare at Payton, sending her an inquiring look. "Sisters before misters," she explained. "Girlfriends should come before boyfriends."

Gemma smiled. "Oh, yes. I completely agree."

They watched as Cal took his turn in the competition, chasing a calf around a series of obstacles. Gemma found the sight of him, bent over the neck of his horse, more than a little stimulating. He seemed so self-assured, so in control—so different from the man who'd shuddered in her arms the night before.

Since she'd returned from Brisbane, things had changed between them. Gemma wasn't sure what had caused the shift in their relationship, but they'd become more open, more honest with each other. She thought it might have begun when she admitted to knowing about the matchmaking service. Up until that point, they'd both avoided any talk of her leaving Kerry Creek.

But now, it had become an accepted fact, inevitable and unchangeable. The clock had begun ticking and they were both powerless to stop it. Gemma knew it was for the best. Her search for the emerald hadn't produced any solid clues. Her last hope was that she might find something in the attic, but Gemma was beginning to question whether she even wanted to continue.

She'd been so sure of herself when she arrived, so single-minded in her purpose that nothing could keep her from her task. In her whole life, all she'd wanted was acceptance from her father, acknowledgment that she did exist and she was his.

But the more time she spent with Cal, the more Gemma realized how her need for a father had affected all her relationships with men. Her mistrust of men in general had simmered beneath the surface, a poison, bubbling up when she began to feel emotions she was unable to explain. But that hadn't happened with Cal. She hadn't felt the need to destroy what they shared simply to maintain control over her own life. She wasn't afraid of him or of her feelings for him.

Perhaps that was because she knew it would all come to an end once she returned to Dublin. The finish had already been determined and she was biding her time until it happened. It was the simplest explanation, yet Gemma didn't believe it.

"Do you ride?" Gemma asked Hayley.

Hayley grinned, nodding. "Like the wind. What about you?"

She wasn't going to lie, even though she wanted to feel like one of the girls. "No. If they did this on bicycles I might give it a go. But horses scare the bleedin' bloomers off me. And I don't care for the way they smell, either." She sighed. "Still, I wish I knew how to ride. Cal seems to be more comfortable on a horse than he does on his feet."

"I could teach you," Payton said.

"Me, too," Hayley offered.

Gemma searched for a polite way to decline, reluctant to confess the depth of her fears. People always seemed to be suspicious of her, unable to understand how she couldn't love a cute dog or a fluffy cat—or a smelly horse. "Cal offered but I didn't want to look like a muppet in front of him, so I begged off. But as long as I'm here, I wouldn't mind trying." Though she attempted to sound enthusiastic, Gemma knew it sounded halfhearted at best.

"It's a date, then," Hayley said, turning to Payton. "You can bring her out to the shack. I'll organize a lunch and then we can ride back together."

"What do you think they're talking about?" Gemma asked, anxious to change the subject.

"Maybe they think we're plotting against them," Payton said.

Brody broke away from his brothers and rode across the stable yard, a wide grin on his handsome face. He tipped his hat as he drew his horse to a halt in front of them. "Ladies, are you having a lovely time?"

"Absolutely," Payton said, sending him a naughty smile.

"What are you doing over here all on your own?"

"Discussing our love of chaps," Gemma offered. "With or without jeans. If I might be so bold, which do you prefer?"

Brody frowned, as if the innuendo didn't register. "Would you ladies like to give it a go? I'm sure the boys would love to see you jump into the competition. And there are prizes to be had for the winners."

Payton crawled over the fence. "I'll try," she volunteered.

"Me, too," Hayley said as she started in Teague's direction.

Gemma maintained her distance on the other side of the fence. "I'm afraid I'll have to sit this one out."

"Come on," Brody insisted. "Cal will ride with you."

There would be no way to hide from her fears. She wanted to run to the bunkhouse and lock herself inside. But everyone else was participating and having a jolly time. She didn't want the stockmen to call her a wowser, the kind of person who sucked all the fun out of a party. "All right."

Reluctantly, she crawled over the fence and headed toward Cal. He slid off his horse and stood beside it. When she got close enough, he slipped his arm around her waist. "You don't have to do this," he murmured. "You don't have anything to prove."

"I know," Gemma said, her voice a bit shaky. But maybe she did want to feel as if she belonged, the way Payton and Hayley did. Maybe, if just for a little while, she'd like to believe Cal might choose her over all the other more suitable matches.

And if she'd already trusted him with her heart and

her body, then why not with her fears? She'd changed since arriving at Kerry Creek and Gemma suspected it was due to Cal. What would happen if she simply gave herself over to him, without questions or reservations. "I suppose I can try."

He bent closer and stared into her eyes. "Really? You're not scared?"

"Terrified," she said. "But I trust you."

Grinning, Cal swung into the saddle, then reached down to grab her arm. "Put your foot in the stirrup," he directed as he slid back.

Clumsily, Gemma did as she was told. He settled her in the saddle and wrapped his arm tightly around her waist. "Oh dear. This is really high. If I fall off, it's going to hurt."

"You won't fall," he said. "I won't let you." He put the reins in her hands. "Just gently tug left to go left and right to go right. It's not tricky."

Gemma nodded. In theory, it was simple enough. But this was a living, breathing creature beneath her, one with a brain of its own. What if Eddie decided he didn't want to play this little game and would rather be running across the countryside at a breakneck speed with her clinging to his back?

"Ready?" Cal asked.

"No. But the sooner this is over, the sooner I can get off this horse."

Cal called to Davey and the jackaroo released a calf from the pen. Gemma glanced over to see Payton and Brody watching them from the other side of the fence, Brody's chin resting on Payton's shoulder. Then the horse suddenly lurched forward and Gemma screamed, startled by the movement.

Cal was shouting directions in her ear but every few seconds, he seemed to want something new. First left, then right, then left again. Though Gemma understood they were trying to drive the calf around the obstacle course of barrels and posts and bales of hay, the horse didn't seem to be interested in cooperating.

After a minute of absolute chaos, Cal reached for the reins, but the stockmen watching on the sidelines shouted their disapproval.

"Drop the reins," he said.

"What?" Gemma wasn't about to let go of the only control they had over the horse. What would stop it from running directly into the fence and tossing them both to the ground? "No, I can't."

"It will be all right," Cal insisted. "I can maneuver him with my knees and feet."

Gemma let the reins slip through her fingers and almost immediately, the horse began to respond. She closed her eyes and held tight to the saddle horn with white-knuckled fingers. Her heart slammed in her chest and she could barely breathe, certain she was about to pitch headlong onto the ground in front of them.

But to her surprise, when she opened her eyes they rode easily around the turn and shooed the calf toward the pen. After it was finally over, she collapsed against Cal, gasping for breath, tears of relief swimming in her eyes.

Though the ride was terrifying, it was also exhilarating. Gemma had never been one to take risks, but now she understood the allure. She hadn't felt this alive since—well, since she and Cal had stripped naked in the bunkhouse and had their way with each other. She could see why the men at Kerry Creek spent so much time on horseback. It worked off a lot of sexual frustration.

"That wasn't so bad," Cal said as he reached down and grabbed the reins. He pulled Eddie to a stop near the gate and slid off, then reached up and grabbed Gemma's waist. She dropped lightly to the ground, but her knees collapsed beneath her and she clutched at his shirt.

"It was like one of those wild rides at an amusement park. Except the guy running it walked away from the controls and the ride was about to go right off the rails."

"I was in control of Eddie the entire time," Cal said. "Didn't you say you trusted me?" He pulled her closer, his hands sliding down to hold her hips against his.

"In most matters," she said. "It's the horse I don't trust."

"Eddie?" He turned to his mount, the horse observing them both with liquid brown eyes. "Hear that, boy?"

The horse responded to Cal's voice and he craned his neck to nuzzle Gemma's shoulder. She jumped back, a tiny scream slipping from her throat. "I think I need to go wash the horse smell off my hands." She sniffed at her palms and wrinkled her nose. "Eddie needs a bath." Gemma pressed her nose against Cal's chest. "And so do you."

"Would you like to take one with me?"

"Now?"

"Later. Tonight. After everyone goes to bed."

The offer was tempting. "The tub upstairs isn't big enough for two," she said.

"I wasn't talking about that tub. We have a hot tub. It's back by the pump house. Very private. Very…hot." He leaned forward and dropped a kiss on her lips. "I'll bring the wine and you bring…your body."

"I don't have a bathing suit," she said.

"You won't need one," Cal replied.

"Oh. I see. This isn't about getting clean."

"Meet me as soon as the boys turn in," he said. "I'll be waiting."

Gemma looked up into his eyes and saw the desire there. They had a busy day ahead of them. After the games, there'd be a barbecue and then the stockmen had insisted on a dance, deciding to take advantage of the female company while they could. Gemma had been charged with inviting both Payton and Hayley. Davey had volunteered to bring the music.

"After the dance," she said.

Cal shook his head. "I think we should just forget the dance. It's just an opportunity for every fella on this station to put his hands all over you. I don't like it."

"You don't like it because you don't want to dance," Gemma said. "You were quite good at it at our camp on the creek."

"That wasn't dancing, that was sex. And I am quite good at that. I just don't think it helps my reputation as a competent boss to be stumbling over my feet in front of my employees."

"I rode that horse. The least you can do is ask me to dance tonight."

"I'll find a way to make it up to you," he said, leaning closer, his voice soft and seductive. "I promise."

A shiver skittered down Gemma's spine as she thought about just what Cal was capable of doing to her. Maybe it was a fair trade. Five minutes on a horse for five hours of incredible pleasure. Life in the outback didn't get much better than that.

THE SUN HAD SET HOURS AGO and the sky was filled with stars, the perfect end to a perfect day. Gemma danced around the yard with Davey, the music softly drifting on the night air. Cal stood on the porch watching them both, his shoulder braced against the corner post, his arms crossed over his chest.

Payton and Brody had retired long ago, silently slipping away to Brody's room upstairs. Hayley and Teague had disappeared shortly afterward, leaving Gemma and Mary to partner with the boys. But now, Gemma was the only female at the party, one beauty among a bunch of drunk fellas.

Gemma looked over Davey's shoulder and gave Cal a little wave, a sign she was ready to leave. God, she was the most beautiful thing he'd ever seen in his life. Every day with her was a revelation, a new realization that he could live a lifetime learning all that there was to know about her.

She seemed happy on Kerry Creek, but Cal had to wonder how much longer she planned to stay. Over the past few days, he'd distracted her from her work on a number of occasions and she didn't kick up a fuss at all.

Cal suspected she'd found all she needed and was stretching out her time so that they might be together a bit longer. But the longer she stayed the more difficult it would be for him to let her go. He'd tried to remain indifferent to his feelings for her, to keep everything in perspective. He'd even pulled out the profiles he'd received from OutbackMates, hoping to convince himself that life would go on after Gemma left.

No matter how he imagined it, Cal couldn't see any way he could have a future with Gemma. Like a puzzle, he'd fit the pieces together in different angles but it always resulted in the two of them living half a world apart.

If he truly cared about her, then he should be willing to make sacrifices. But he couldn't leave Kerry Creek. This station was his life, his dream. No woman was worth giving that up, even a woman he loved. Cal was willing to spend the rest of his life alone before considering that option.

The song ended and Davey stepped back, then gave Gemma a chaste peck on the cheek. It was already past ten and everyone needed to be up again in six hours, including him. And he had at least an hour or two planned with Gemma.

"Last dance," he said to the boys. "And I'm claiming this one. I'll see you fellas in the morning."

The stockmen wandered off into the darkness and Gemma stepped into Cal's arms. She had put on her jacket against the chill of the evening and he slipped his hands beneath it, smoothing them over her backside. "I've been waiting for this all night."

"I suppose you think I'm going home with you since you're the only guy left at the dance?"

"Yeah, I was counting on it," Cal said with a chuckle.

"I don't know," Gemma said. "I'm thinking I should have taken Davey up on his offer."

Cal stopped dancing and looked down at her. "Davey propositioned you? What did he say?"

"He said I was a bit of alright and if I got bored with you, I ought to give him a chance. I told him he might be a little young for me and he told me age was a state of mind."

"Davey said that?" Cal chuckled. "Not a bad line. So are you going to consider his offer?"

"That depends upon your offer. What are you going to do for me, Cal Quinn?"

Her words were a teasing challenge, but Cal could certainly best a nineteen-year-old jackaroo when it came to seduction. He laced his fingers through hers and pulled her along toward the pump house. "I'm going to get you naked and have my way with you," he said. "I'm going to touch you in all the places you love to be touched. And I'm going to make you tremble, the way you did last night."

Gemma let go of his hand and backed away from him, tugging off her cardie and tossing it his way. "You're going to have to catch me first," she said.

With a growl, Cal ran after her. They finally came together on the far side of the pump house, a low building that housed the main well for the homestead. Cal had originally ordered the hot tub to help Brody with his rehab after his motorcycle accident. It had gone largely unused, except by the stockmen after long stretches in the saddle. But now he considered it a prudent purchase.

He pulled off the vinyl cover and a cloud of moisture rose into the cool air. Then he pulled his shirt over his head and tossed it aside. "Now you," he said, waiting for her to remove another article of clothing.

Gemma tugged off her shoe, then held it up to him. "A girl could get very bored at this pace," she said.

"Then let me move things along." He reached for her and in a flurry of movement, they tore at each other's clothes until they were both naked.

"I'm getting used to this," she said. "I might never put clothes on again."

Cal took her hand and helped her into the tub. Slowly, they sank down into the bubbling water, their bodies intertwined. "Oh, this is lovely," Gemma murmured, closing her eyes and tipping her head back. "My bum is a bit sore from that horse ride," she said. "Doesn't yours ever get sore riding all day long?"

"Why don't I do something about that." He slowly smoothed his hands over her backside, gently kneading the sweet flesh as her hips shifted against his. "When I had this installed, I never thought I'd be enjoying it with a woman. It was for Brody, after his accident."

"It's perfect," she said, pressing a kiss to his damp shoulder. "Very relaxing."

Cal ran his finger over her cheek and smiled. "Now that I have you here, I want to ask you something."

Gemma snuggled up next to him, her legs straddling his hips. "Ask away."

"I'm not sure how to put this. Is there…do you have a…someone back in Ireland? A fella? In your life?"

She pulled away from him, a frown creasing her brow. "No? Did you think I did?"

"No," Cal said. "Well, maybe. It just didn't figure."

"What do you mean?"

"You're beautiful and perfect. And you're smart and you know how to make a bloke feel real good—not in a sexual way, but…well, happy. Content. Why hasn't some guy claimed you for himself?"

"Claimed me?"

Callum sighed. "You know what I mean. I'm not the best with words, but you're smart enough to understand what I'm trying to say. Why are you still alone?"

Gemma shrugged. "I don't want to be married. I'm happy with my life the way it is." She paused. "Callum, I'm not perfect. Far from it. I have a lot of insecurities that I keep very well hidden. Don't make me out to be some extraordinary woman."

"You might not think you're perfect," Callum said. "But you're perfect for me." He reached up and ran his thumb over her bottom lip. "I want you to move into the house with me. Payton is staying in Brody's room now and there's no reason why you should be living in the bunkhouse. I have a big, comfortable bed and a door with a strong lock."

Gemma slowly drifted back to the other side of the tub. "You have all sorts of plans, don't you?"

He watched her, the underwater lights illuminating her pretty features. "It's simple, really. Either you want to be with me or you don't. I don't want to waste the time we have left." He held out his hand. "But if you do, no worries."

She studied him for a long moment, her face etched with indecision. Cal said a silent prayer, grateful she was considering his offer and hoping she'd accept. He wouldn't have any regrets about what he'd done. He'd asked and if she refused, he'd accept her decision.

But if she moved into his room, then he was going to spend every night lost in the body of this beautiful woman who had dropped into his life in the middle of a lonely Australian winter. She was a gift and he wouldn't take her for granted.

7

GEMMA AWOKE SLOWLY, AWARE FIRST of the warm, naked body lying beside her. She nuzzled her face into Cal's shoulder and sighed softly. Cal had been right. She belonged here in his room. Her bed in the bunkhouse was far too small for the two of them and his was…just right.

Though sleeping in his room did feel a bit naughty, Gemma had decided to toss aside her inhibitions and enjoy their relationship for what it was—wildly satisfying and intensely exciting. She would enjoy it while it lasted.

What in the world did she have to lose? Summer in Dublin was pleasant, but she'd spend it at the library or in her office, doing work that could be better left for another time. Here, on Kerry Creek, she had passion and desire, a man to see to her every sexual need. A girl would have to be thick as a ditch to walk away from that.

Gemma closed her eyes, smiling to herself. She was glad she hadn't told him about the emerald. She'd destroyed many relationships in the past, but she wasn't going to ruin this one. They'd been together a little more than a week. And yet, Gemma already knew what she and Cal shared was special.

The depth of her feelings for him frightened her as much as that ride on Eddie. What was she supposed to do with all this? She'd avoided even thinking of anything permanent with him. Because she knew she would go home, leaving him behind.

Strangely enough, her escape clause gave her the freedom to stay and explore this odd new emotional attachment. He was safe, yet he was oh, so dangerous at the same time.

Gemma pushed aside the bed covers and sat up, brushing her hair over her shoulder. She watched him sleep, his features relaxed, almost boyish. Her gaze drifted down, to the body that had become hers by default. Cal was a beautiful man in the physical sense of the word but her attraction to him was well beyond appreciation for a gorgeous form. She loved his heart and his humor, the way he looked at her, as if she were the most beautiful woman in the world.

Gemma reached out and ran her hand along his arm, from his shoulder to his wrist. A feeling of utter amazement washed over her as she remembered the way he'd touched her the night before. Had they really only known each other for a week? How was it possible that their bodies had become so attuned to each other?

She bent over and pressed a kiss to his chest, her hair falling around her face. Cal stirred and a moment later, his fingers touched her cheek. She turned to find him staring at her in the early morning light, a sleepy smile on his face.

"Morning," he said.

Gemma grinned. "For some of us, that might be debatable. I'm not usually awake this early."

He groaned and rolled onto his side, then pulled the pillow over his face. "Then go back to sleep. I don't have to get up for a while."

"You don't?"

"One of the benefits of being boss cocky. Besides, the boys will roll out of their bunks a bit later this morning, too, after all the beer they consumed yesterday."

Gemma snuggled against his chest, her fingers toying with the soft trail of hair that ran from his collarbone to his belly. "I had a good time yesterday," she said. "I was thinking if I stay for a while, I should probably try riding again."

He pushed up on his elbow. "Are you going to stay?"

"Maybe," she said. "I think I will. A bit longer, at least. Until the end of the month."

He ran his hand through her hair, brushing the tangled curls from her face. "That's good. That's very good." He laughed, not able to contain his delight. He grabbed her arms and pulled her up alongside him, dragging her into a long, delicious kiss. "We'll have fun," he said. "By the time mustering starts, you'll be riding as well as a jackaroo. And I think we should take some time away from the station. I can spare a few days here and there. We'll have Teague fly us somewhere interesting." He kissed her again. "You really want to learn to ride?"

"Maybe we could try riding together again, without chasing that little cow around the cattle yard?"

"That was a calf," he said.

"I know."

"And that's pretty much what mustering is. Chasing cattle around the station. But you wouldn't be up for mustering, a city girl like you. It's dirty work. I'm not sure you're cut out for it. You'd best stay in the house baking biscuits with Mary."

Gemma recognized reverse psychology when she saw it. "And you'd better get used to sleeping alone."

He growled softly, then rolled her on top of him, their naked limbs tangling in the sheets. "That's not going to happen," he said. "Sleeping arrangements are non-negotiable."

"So, what is this? What do we call it?" Gemma asked. "Is it an affair?"

"Doesn't that usually involve some form of cheating?"

"No. It can also mean a short-term arrangement. With no strings attached."

"Is that all right with you?" he asked.

Gemma didn't hesitate. "Yes," she said. "But that's all it can be. Nothing more. Agreed?"

"Agreed," Cal said. "Now, can we go back to sleep?" He twisted to see the clock on the bedside table. "I've had two hours rest and if I don't get at least four, I'm buggered for the next day."

Gemma wriggled on top of him. "But I'm not tired." She straddled his hips and sat up, moving deliberately to tease at his desire. "You were much more attentive to my needs when we weren't sleeping together. See what this has done to our relationship already? It's like my mother always told me—that old cow and milk proverb."

"What proverb is that?" Cal asked, his hands moving to her waist.

"Why sleep with the cow when you can buy the milk for free?" she whispered. Gemma leaned close and brushed a kiss across his mouth.

"I don't think that's it," he said. "But I do get your point. So, am I the cow? Or am I the milk."

"Neither." She slid down and pressed a kiss to his belly. "Where do you keep the condoms?"

Not waiting for a reply, Gemma reached over to pull out the drawer on the bedside table. She withdrew a crumpled paper and Cal quickly grabbed it from her. When she grabbed it back, she found an advert for Out-backMates. "Is this it?"

Cal groaned. "It was a silly idea. I don't know how I ever thought I'd find a woman that way." He wadded the paper into a ball and threw it across the room. "The condoms aren't in there. Since I've never had a woman in this room, there's no reason to keep them beside the bed."

"You've never had a woman in your bed?"

Cal shook his head. "You're the first. Until you got to the station, I lived like a monk." He pointed to the bookcase on the far wall. "They're behind the murder mysteries," he said.

Gemma crawled out of bed and retrieved the box, then watched him from across the room. She'd never lived with a man before, at least not for more than a few nights at a time. Was she ready for this? It went against all of her instincts, her need to protect herself from any long-term commitments. Still, if it became too much to handle, she could always move back into the bunk-house.

"Maybe we should go back to sleep," she teased as

she walked to the side of the bed. Her gaze drifted down to his shaft, now hard and ready. "I can see you're tired."

Cal grabbed her hand and yanked her back into bed, rolling on top of her and pinning her hands at her sides. "I'm definitely not tired," he said, moving against her.

Gemma moaned softly as his shaft teased at the folds of her sex. She brought her legs up and the next time he moved, he slipped inside of her for a moment, before drawing back.

"Don't do that to me," he warned.

"It's all right," Gemma said.

"No, it's not."

Though Gemma was a good Irish Catholic girl, she didn't follow the church's edicts on birth control. The moment she'd become sexually active, she'd found a doctor to prescribe the pill and she hadn't stopped taking them since. She wouldn't make the same mistake her mother had, even though she'd been the result of that mistake. Gemma wanted control of her future and that future didn't include any unexpected babies with reluctant fathers.

"I've been safe," she said. "Have you?"

"Yes." He released a tightly held breath as she sank down on top of him.

Gemma splayed her fingers across his chest, closing her eyes as he penetrated deeper. And when he was buried inside her, she stayed still for a long moment, enjoying the warmth of him filling her.

"I've never done this before," he whispered as she began to move above him. "It feels different."

Gemma smiled. "It's nice."

His hand cupped her breast and Cal rubbed his thumb across her nipple, drawing it to a tight peak. She closed her eyes again, allowing her mind to drift, focusing on the feeling of his touch. But when his fingers found the spot where they were joined, Gemma gasped softly.

Movements that had once been slow and easy now grew faster and more determined. She rocked above him, each thrust bringing her closer to the edge. It was so simple to just let go, to lose control. But as the first spasm struck, Gemma felt a tiny sliver of fear prick at her pleasure.

Would she have the strength to walk away? Would the feelings that seemed to overwhelm her at times grow so strong that they'd be impossible to ignore? She didn't want to fall in love. Love only made a mess of people's lives.

And yet, as her orgasm slowly subsided and his began, Gemma realized she'd already allowed herself to get closer to Cal than she had with any other man. The bond between them was simple, yet incredibly strong. And breaking it might just break her heart, as well. Maybe she already loved him and she didn't even know.

CAL STOOD ON THE PORCH and watched as Brody rode off in a cloud of dust. He nodded at Teague as his brother hopped behind the wheel of his Range Rover. The screen door squeaked and Gemma stepped out, staring at him, a confused expression on her face.

"What's going on?" she asked.

"A private investigator just showed up looking for Payton. He's in the parlor right now."

"What does he want with Payton?"

"I don't know. Brody wouldn't say. He talked Teague into flying them both off the station. They're headed out to the airstrip now." He took her hand. "Come on. We better find a way to get rid of him."

When they returned to the parlor, the detective was standing near the mantel, examining the family photos displayed there. "You might as well tell me where she is," he said. "I'm going to find her sooner or later."

"Like Teague told you, she was here and then she left. Gemma knows." He gave her hand a squeeze. "Tell him."

"She was here. She lived with me in the bunkhouse. But she's not there anymore. She left."

"How long ago?"

"Days?" Gemma said. "I'm really not sure. I think it was the day after we got back from Brisbane, wasn't it?"

With a soft curse, the man picked up his hat and strode to the door. "You're not helping her." Cal made a move to follow him, but the man held up his hand. "I can find my own way out."

A few moments later, they heard the screen door slam. Gemma slowly sat down on the sofa. "What was that all about? What do you think she did that they'd send a detective looking for her? You don't think she's a criminal, do you?"

"I don't know," Cal said.

"She told me she'd run out on her wedding. Do you

think they're trying to fetch her back and make her marry the bloke? Is that legal?"

"Of course not. But this is what comes from keeping secrets. How long have you known about this wedding of hers?"

Gemma shrugged, an uneasy expression on her face. "Since last week sometime. I didn't think it was that important."

"What if she's married? What if Brody has got himself all twisted up with some deranged husband searching for his missing wife?"

"No," Gemma replied, shaking her head. "I'm sure she's not married. She would have said something about that. She ran away before the wedding took place."

"This is why I hate secrets." Cal sat down beside her and grabbed her hand. "This one little thing could ruin everything Brody has invested in this girl. I knew she was trouble from the moment she walked onto this station. I should have trusted my instinct and sent her—"

"She's not trouble," Gemma insisted. "I know Payton. She cares about Brody. She'd never hurt him. Just like I'd never hurt you."

"You're not keeping any secrets," he said. He glanced over at her only to see a pained expression cross her features. "You aren't, right?"

"Everyone has secrets," Gemma said. "There are things we keep to ourselves, things we don't allow others to see. There's nothing wrong with that."

"I think honesty is more important than anything. If you don't have that, then sooner or later, it all falls apart."

She stared at him for a long moment, then shook her head. "No. What if keeping a secret prevents you from hurting someone? Isn't that a reason to stay quiet? What if someone said something terrible about one of your brothers, something you knew would hurt them? Wouldn't you keep that secret?"

"Why are we speaking in hypothetical terms, Gemma? If you have something to tell me, just say it. Nothing will change how I feel about you."

"No," she said in an emotionless voice. "I can't. I don't want to."

Cal felt a knot of fear tighten in his gut. What was she going to say? Had she lied to him about being involved with someone else? Hell, what difference did that make either way? She was with him now, not with some nameless, faceless Irishman. "Gemma, we don't have a lot of time together. We might as well be completely honest with each other."

She watched him with suspicious eyes. "You promise not to get angry?"

"As long as you don't tell me you have a husband and three children back in Dublin."

"No," Gemma said. "No children, no husband."

"Then how can I possibly get angry."

She took a deep breath. "It's a very complicated story and I need to tell it carefully, or you won't understand. And I need you to understand." She took a deep breath. "I'm not a genealogist, Cal. I didn't come here to research your family history. There is no rich Quinn relative paying me to do this. That was just a story I told so you'd let me stay at the station."

"Why would you lie?" Cal asked.

"Because I was afraid if I told you the real reason I was here, you'd send me away." She paused. "Have you ever heard of the Emerald of Eire?"

Cal shrugged. "Sure. Everyone has heard of that."

Gemma stared at him, wide-eyed and speechless. "You know where it is, then?" she finally said.

"Ireland? Of course."

"No the Emerald of—"

"The Emerald Isle. That's Ireland. What does this have to do with anything?"

"No, you don't understand. The Emerald of Eire is an actual emerald. A huge stone. A precious jewel. It belonged to my father's family."

"I thought you didn't know your father." She was talking in riddles. Emeralds and her father and… What did any of that have to do with them?

"I don't know him. Not really. The Emerald of Eire was stolen by your ancestor, Crevan Quinn, from my ancestor, Stanton Parnell. There's a good chance Crevan brought it here to Australia. I think it might be somewhere in this house or on this station right now. I came here to get it back."

Cal shook his head. This was her secret? With her nervous preamble, he'd been expecting something more disturbing. "That's why you came here? For some old jewelry?"

"This is a huge emerald. It's worth a half million British pounds. I wanted to find it and take it back to my father. In exchange, I'd insist he recognize me as his daughter."

"That's not much of a secret," Cal said. "Why didn't

you just tell me up front what you wanted? I could have helped you look for it."

"You're just going to give me the emerald?"

"It belongs to your family, doesn't it?"

"Well, my family might have a problem proving that after all this time. And they say possession is nine-tenths of the law."

"So it might belong to the Quinns?"

"You could make a case in court. Or you could keep the jewel and sell it. Of course, an emerald that size would prompt a few questions and…" She paused. "I need that emerald, Cal. As a bargaining tool. With my fair share of the Parnell trust, I can make sure my mother lives comfortably."

"How do you know it's here?"

"The portrait," Gemma said. "It's embedded in the head of Crevan's walking stick. He had it when that portrait was painted. We'll just have to figure out where it went from there."

"And what if I do have this emerald?"

"Do you?" She held her breath and Cal could see what it was costing her to remain calm.

Of course he didn't have it. But there was another possibility, a possibility that he didn't care for in the least. "What if you find proof that Crevan sold it?"

"I don't know all the legalities," she said. "I suppose there would need to be some form of restitution. It is stolen property."

Callum knew where this was going. "I don't have a half million pounds."

"I'm sure you wouldn't owe that. But if Crevan used

the emerald to buy Kerry Creek, then there might be a problem. But that's just a guess. I don't know. I guess I didn't really think that part out very thoroughly."

He stood up, his hands clenched at his sides. This was exactly what he'd warned her about. Secrets always seemed to be more damaging the longer they were kept. And this one had the capability of turning his life upside down. "You'd better find that emerald," he warned. "Because there is no way I'd give up any part of Kerry Creek because of something that happened a hundred years ago."

"A hundred and fifty," she corrected.

Cal grabbed his hat from the end of the sofa, holding tight to his temper. "I need to get to work," he said.

"Don't worry," Gemma insisted. "I'd never let anyone take any part of the station away from you."

"You wouldn't have any say in the matter," he said. "That stone does exist. It was on that walking stick. And as long as anyone in your family remembers it, it's always going to be hanging over my family's head. You need to find it, Gemma, and then you need to take it back to Ireland."

She reached out and grabbed his arm. "I wanted to tell you earlier, but after a while, it didn't make any difference. I started to care more about you than the emerald. That's a very big step for me." The more she talked, the more distant he became. "Don't just walk out, Callum. I need you to understand. And to forgive me."

"We'll talk later," Cal said. "I'm tired and cranky. Better to leave it for another time."

As he walked out of the library, Cal pulled the door

shut behind him. He drew a deep breath and closed his eyes, cursing beneath his breath. He should have expected something like this. Her story had been suspect from the start, but he'd let his attraction to her override his common sense. And she'd been playing him all along. Maybe sleeping with him was all part of her plan, too. How far was she willing to go to get what she wanted?

And how easy would it be to forgive her? He didn't love her. Hell, he barely knew her and this incident proved his point. She was a liar. And had she found the emerald, he suspected she would have made herself a thief, as well.

He paused. Well, not exactly a thief, since technically, she'd be taking something that had been stolen from her family in the first place. Hell, he could work out the moral ramifications later. Right now, he needed hard work, exhausting work, work designed to drive thoughts of Gemma right out of his head. Once he'd done that, he could worry about what this meant to Kerry Creek.

GEMMA PEERED THROUGH bleary eyes at the journal she was reading. Over the past week, she'd gone through every last trunk in the attic, had removed every book from the shelves in the library, had searched very nook and cranny in the house. If she hadn't found any information about the emerald by now, then she was probably at a dead end.

She'd spent two days in Sydney, searching through the papers of the portrait artist, looking for clues there. After that, she'd been to the land offices in Brisbane and looked through all the deeds to the property that had been added to Kerry Creek over the years. She'd picked through expense ledgers and yellowing receipts, looking for a large infusion of cash from the sale of the stone.

"Nothing," she murmured. "There's nothing here."

In truth, she wanted to put an end to this. Since she'd told Cal the real reason for her trip to Kerry Creek, he'd become detached, maintaining a chilly reserve whenever they spoke. He'd insisted she finish her research, concerned that the emerald was a dark cloud hanging over the station.

Whenever she saw him, at meals and sometimes in passing, he'd force a smile and give her a benign greeting before finding some silly excuse not to carry on a conversation. She'd thought about sneaking up to his room in the middle of the night and forcing the issue. But she was afraid of rejection. Besides, it would be much easier for her to walk away if their relationship was beyond repair.

He seemed so tired, so spent, with dark circles smudging the skin beneath his eyes. She wanted to believe it was station business that was weighing on his mind—or the land dispute with Hayley's grandfather—or Brody and Payton's sudden departure with a private investigator on their trail.

They hadn't touched each other since she'd revealed her secret. Eight days and eight nights to be exact. She kept telling herself she was only at the station because she wanted to find the emerald—for him, not her father. But above all, Gemma was hoping they might be able to smooth over the rift between them.

How much longer could this go on? If their relationship was irreparable, then she ought to go home and save herself any more humiliation. The worst thing imaginable would be if he asked her to leave. Gemma wasn't sure she'd be able to handle that.

Funny how things had changed in her life. She was always the one who walked away from men, the one who called a swift and painless end to her romances. And now, she was hanging on for dear life, hoping that Cal would want her again.

"You're pathetic," Gemma muttered. "Grow a spine and go home."

A soft knock sounded on the door and a moment later, Mary stepped through with a tray of tea and toast. "I thought you might like something. You haven't had breakfast."

"Thank you," Gemma said. "I am hungry."

Mary set the tray down, then poured a cup of tea. "I've noticed you and Cal haven't been getting along lately. And you've been staying away from the dinner table."

"It's complicated," Gemma said. "But it's all right. I'm going to be leaving soon, so it's better our romance has…fizzled out."

Mary set the tea down in front of Gemma, then took a chair on the other side of the desk. "Cal takes his responsibilities here very seriously. And sometimes they weigh heavily on him. With Harry Fraser and this land dispute starting up again, he feels…" She paused, searching for the right word. "Threatened. He's not happy about Teague and Hayley. Brody is on the run from the private investigator who has been chasing Payton. And mustering begins in a few weeks."

"And I've just added to all his troubles."

"Yes, but not in the way you think."

"What do you mean?"

"Cal has always tried to control everything around him."

Gemma giggled. "I know how that is. I do the same thing."

"And when you walked into his life, he learned that sometimes it's just fine to forget the plans. I think he's fallen in love with you, Gemma. He just hasn't figured it out yet."

"No," Gemma said. "We're…it's just been…it's not supposed to last. We both knew that."

"Who said it's not supposed to last? If you want it to last, it will."

"But…I don't," Gemma said. The minute the words were out of her mouth, she knew they were a lie. But what did that mean? Was she really hoping that they could make this work?

"Then don't draw this out any longer than you have to," Mary said. "Leave Kerry Creek and let him get on with his life."

"Mary!" The sound of Cal's shout echoed through the house. "Mary!"

"I'm in the library," Mary called.

A few seconds later, Cal appeared at the door. "You need to come, right away. Harry Fraser just showed up in the yard and he's fallen off his horse. He's lying in the dirt outside."

Mary stood up and hurried out of the library. Cal's gaze locked with Gemma's and she stepped from behind the desk. "Did you call anyone?" she asked.

"The air ambulance is on the way. But the old man wants to get back on his horse. He can't walk. I think he's broken his leg."

Gemma grabbed his hand and hurried back through the house. When they got to the porch, she saw the stockmen gathered around Harry. He was shouting at them, waving his arm as he struggled to sit up. Mary knelt beside him, trying to calm him down.

"Did you call Hayley?" Gemma asked.

"She's somewhere with Teague, I think. They flew out a few days ago. I don't know where they went."

"See if you can find her. Call the vet he works with."

"Doc Daley," Cal said.

"He probably left a number with him. I'll help Mary."

Gemma ran down the steps and joined the house-keeper. "Boys, why don't you get back to work," she said. "Mary and I can take care of this." When they didn't move, she turned Davey around and gave him a gentle shove. "Go," she said in a low voice. "You're just making him more upset."

Slowly, the boys scattered. Gemma squatted down beside the old man. "We're going to call Hayley," she said. "Stay still. You'll be fine."

"Put me back on my damn horse," he demanded.

"No," Gemma replied in a firm voice. "I don't think you can get back on your horse right now."

"Who are you?" he asked.

"Just a visitor here," Gemma said. "My name is Gemma."

"Keep those Quinns away from me," he muttered. "They'd sooner kill me than help me."

"Why don't you tell me what hurts," she said.

"My hip." He groaned as he tried to move again. "It hurts like hell."

"Mary, why don't you get some ice and a pillow for Mr. Fraser's head. So he can lie back and relax. And can you ask Cal to take care of his horse, please?"

"Don't touch that horse," Harry warned.

"We'll just have Cal give him some water."

"Her," Harry said. "It's a mare."

"Oh. See, well, that's interesting. I don't know much about horses. In fact, I'm frightened of them. For just this reason. Is this the first time you've fallen?"

"No," Harry said. "I had a bad fall about ten years back. Broke my arm."

"I suppose it was difficult to work your station with a broken arm," Gemma commented. "How did you manage that?"

Over the next hour, Gemma kept Harry calm and alert with an endless stream of conversation. Mary went back and forth between the doctor on the phone and fetching fresh ice to put on Harry's hip.

The helicopter flew low over the homestead before it landed just beyond the house. Gemma held Harry's hand as the medics attended to him. They splinted his legs together, then carefully put him on a stretcher. As they moved him to the helicopter, she walked along beside him, keeping up a running commentary.

Cal was waiting for her when she returned to the house, standing on the porch, his expression cloudy, his mouth set in a grim line. He held out his hand as she climbed the steps. "Come with me," he said.

She followed him upstairs to his room and when he got there, Cal slammed the door behind them. He turned to her, cradled her face between his hands and kissed her. The kiss took her by surprise and she drew in a sharp breath. But then, as her mouth molded against his, Gemma sighed. They'd seemed miles apart just this morning and now, a single kiss was all it took to bring them back together again.

"I'm sorry," he murmured. "I've been such an ass."

"No," she said. "I'm the one who's sorry. It was a foolish plan for a foolish reason. I should never have come here."

"Don't say that," Cal said. "I'm glad you're here. I could never have handled Harry like that. You just kept him calm and distracted." He paused. "The last week has been sheer hell, Gemma. I've tried to stop caring about you, but I can't."

He kissed her again, his hands running over her body as if trying to make up for the week they'd lost. Before long they were tugging at each other's clothes, the passion crackling between them. When they were left in just their underwear, they tumbled onto the bed, lost in an endless kiss.

Gemma hadn't realized how much this desire had become a necessary part of her life. Touching Cal, tasting Cal, it was as natural as breathing. Even after everything that had happened, all the distance between them, Gemma felt as though they were moving toward something deeper, more lasting.

Was she fooling herself? They'd known each other for exactly eighteen days. They had everything working against them and yet, it was becoming more difficult every day to ignore the intensity of her emotions.

Gemma had protected her heart for so long, encased it in a hard shell that no one could penetrate. But then she'd come here, to Kerry Creek, and forgotten to put up her defenses. By the time she remembered, it was too late.

"No one knows I came here for the emerald," she murmured. "Just you and me. If we don't find it, sooner or later, the story will be lost to history. People will forget and Kerry Creek will be safe."

"Another secret?" he asked.

Gemma nodded. "But this is a good secret. One worth keeping."

There was a way to move into the future with Cal. But no matter how she looked at it, it would involve her staying at Kerry Creek, giving up everything in Dublin, her friends, her job, her home. The thought was overwhelming.

She didn't want to think about that now. All she wanted was to lose herself in Cal. She could sort the rest out later.

8

"ALL RIGHT. I'LL SELL YOU the land," Cal said. "I'll call our solicitor and have him draw up some sort of agreement. But the next time anything comes to a vote, you vote with me."

Cal couldn't believe what Teague had convinced him to do. After all this time arguing a land dispute with Harry Fraser, after years of fighting between the two families, Cal had just approved a peace treaty.

Though on the surface it seemed like a crazy idea, Cal had to trust that Teague knew what he was doing. Harry was in the hospital, refusing surgery for his broken hip. The prognosis was grim and Hayley was desperate to change his mind. Giving Harry the land would give him a reason to live, or so Teague claimed.

"Thank you," his brother said, smiling. "This will all turn out in the end. I promise."

Cal groaned inwardly. This was crazy, but he had to trust his brother. "I'm going to hold you to that promise. Now, get the hell out of my office. And tell Gemma she can come in."

"If it's possible, I'd like the agreement today. Before I head to Brisbane."

Cal frowned. "Today? Why today?"

"Because I need it today," Teague insisted, looking at his watch. "In the next hour or two would be good." He stood and moved to the door. "Thanks, Cal. I owe you. Free vet services for the next fifty years."

"That would about cover it," Cal muttered. "As long as you throw in ownership of the plane, too."

Callum leaned back in his chair, waiting for Gemma to return. She had poked her head in the library looking for him a few minutes ago, but excused herself when she realized he and Teague were in the midst of a serious conversation. But he needed her now, to tell him that he wasn't a gullible fool to have agreed to Teague's plans.

Odd how that all he seemed to need in life was her approval. He didn't care about anything else except Gemma. The station was still important, but it was just land and buildings, possessions that, though an integral part of his life, didn't have the capacity to make him happy. Not the way Gemma did.

Cal reached for the phone and placed a call to his solicitor. Though he carefully explained the deal he and Teague had reached, requesting a letter of agreement for the land deal, his solicitor spent five minutes arguing against it. Cal finally got a promise for an e-mail copy of the agreement, sent within the hour. That done, he turned on his computer and waited while the dial-up modem made the connection.

His e-mail account boasted five new letters, four more than he usually got in a week. He opened the mailbox, expecting to find a notification of shipping confirmation on the windmill parts he'd ordered. Instead he noticed a series of three notes from OutbackMates.

Cal opened the first to find a letter from one of the three women the service had chosen for him. Sylvie Monroe. Cursing softly, he quickly closed it. Had he misunderstood the rules? Wasn't he supposed to make the first move? Maybe these women had grown impatient waiting. After all, it had been three weeks. "Hell," he muttered. Cal already had enough to deal with and now this?

"Hi."

He glanced up to see Gemma standing at the door. She wore a pale green cotton dress that set off her eyes, eyes that he loved staring into. Cal quickly turned off his computer. "Hi."

"Mary and I baked some bickies. Chocolate chip. They're still warm. Would you like some?"

"Sure," Cal said.

"I sent some with Teague for Hayley." She took a step into the room. "Did he say how her grandfather was doing? I didn't want to press him for details."

"He has a broken hip and they want to do surgery. But he's refusing. So, Teague is taking him something that might change his mind. Quinn land."

Gemma's eyes went wide. "You're giving him the land you've been fighting over?"

Cal nodded. "Tell me I'm not losing my mind, Gemma. This seems so important to Teague. And he does have a third share in the station."

"No," Gemma said, slowly approaching the desk. "I

don't think you're crazy. It's just land. And Teague is your brother."

Cal chuckled. "Yeah. A brother who just convinced me to give away the land with the best water bore on Kerry Creek. But Teague wanted to do this for Hayley and for her grandfather."

"He loves her," Gemma said.

"Yeah, I believe he does. I think he always has, all these years. It's rather amazing if you think of it. Almost ten years apart and their feelings survived."

She circled the desk and wrapped her arms around his neck. "You're a good man, Cal." Gemma sat down on his lap, throwing her legs over the arm of his chair. "Did you notice how tidy the library is?"

He nodded. "Are you finished with your work?"

Gemma nodded, her mood turning serious. "I didn't find anything, Cal. If Crevan brought the emerald here, then he must have buried it somewhere in the outback. Because it's not in the house."

"Maybe he did bury it," Cal said. "Remember that story I told you about? The one about buried treasure on the station. You could probably ask my father. He might know more."

"Maybe when you decide to tear down a wall or pull up a floor, you'll find it hidden away. Or maybe, Crevan never had it in the first place. From everything I've read about him, he had an odd sense of humor. Maybe painting the emerald into the portrait was his idea of a joke."

"Or a clue?" Cal asked.

Gemma shook her head. "No. The emerald needs to

remain lost. It's better for you and better for me." She drew a deep breath. "And I need to get home," she added softly.

Cal leaned back in his chair. He knew this was coming, yet he hadn't decided how to handle it. His first instinct was to beg her to stay, to convince her they couldn't live without each other. But Cal knew as well as she did that begging would get them nowhere.

The feelings that had brought them this far just weren't strong enough to last forever. Sure, he wanted to believe that desire was the only thing needed for two people to fall in love. But there were many more practical considerations, as well—like living on the same bloody continent.

"When are you going to go?"

"I thought I'd stay another week, if it was all right with you," she suggested. "We haven't spent much time together lately. And I was hoping you'd teach me to ride. Unless, of course, you're too busy."

"No. Another week would be perfect," he said, relief washing over him. "I can take some time away from the station. Maybe we can see some of the sights in Queensland. We could go to the wineries at Darling Downs. Or go camping at Carnarvon. Or we could go to Brisbane and spend some time at the beach. What would you like to do?"

"I think I'd like to stay here," Gemma said. "We could go back to that spot on Kerry Creek and spend a night or two."

Cal reached out and took her hand in his, toying with her fingers. "If you're going to stay for another week, then I want you to stay with me. In my room."

She nodded. "All right. With Payton gone, the bunkhouse has been a bit lonely."

It was the most he could hope for. One more week with Gemma, in his life and in his bed. He intended to make every single minute count. And after she left, he'd do his best to forget that he'd just lost the best thing that had ever happened to him.

"NOW YOU'RE RIDING," Cal called. "Just relax. See if you can move with the horse. Raise yourself up just a bit in the stirrups."

Gemma did as she was told. The horse, Tibby, was a gentle mare that Cal had chosen especially for her. Unlike the others, Tibby wasn't in foal, which made Gemma feel a bit sorry for her. She'd imagined all sorts of feelings going on in the horse's head and from the moment she touched Tibby's velvety muzzle, they'd made a connection. This was an animal she could trust.

Cal held on to a lead he'd fastened to Tibby's bridle, keeping the horse running in a wide circle around him. "Do you want to try a little faster gait?" he asked.

"No," Gemma said. "Tibby is tired."

"Don't worry. You're doing very well. Give it a try."

"All right," Gemma said, preparing herself for the fall that would soon follow. She'd nearly fallen twice already, but Cal had caught her before she hit the ground. She was counting on that again. "If I scream, you have to slow her down."

He clucked his tongue and slapped the ground with the end of the lead. Tibby responded immediately, picking up her pace. Gemma leaned forward and lifted up in the stirrups and to her surprise, she moved along with the horse's rhythm, as if they were of one mind. "I know what you mean," she called to Cal. "This is it. It's not so hard."

But a moment later, she fell out of the cadence and found herself bouncing against the saddle, each step jolting her. Cal slowed the horse to a walk. "That was good," he said.

Gemma grinned. "It was good." She leaned over and patted Tibby's neck. "Good girl." Tibby nodded her head and Gemma gently pulled her to a stop. "I think I'm going to need an hour in the hot tub. My bum is going to be sore again."

For the past week, she'd had a riding lesson every day and to her surprise, she'd managed to conquer her fears—at least some of them. She wasn't afraid of being bitten, she'd gotten used to the smell, and she'd even reconciled the distance between the top of the horse and the ground as survivable in a fall.

What she hadn't reconciled were her feelings for Cal. It had been exactly a week since she'd agreed to stay. Yet neither one of them had brought up her leaving. They both seemed content to extend the vacation, day by day, without comment or question.

But avoiding the topic of their parting wasn't doing either of them any good. It just gave them an excuse to pretend as if there were nothing standing between them. It gave them an excuse to fall more deeply in love. And that would only make it more difficult in the end.

"Again," she said. "I want to go again."

"Riding is very good exercise," he said. "Good for the thighs."

"I do love your thighs," Gemma teased. She noticed Mary approaching the stable yard and gave her a wave. "Here's Mary and she doesn't look very happy. Have we missed lunch?" Gemma stood up in the stirrups. "Mary, I'm riding!"

Mary stopped at the fence. "Gemma, you have a phone call. It's urgent. You need to come right away."

"Who is it? Is it Payton? Did the private investigator find them?"

"It's not Payton. It's your mother," Mary said, a worried expression on her face. "She says it's an emergency."

Gemma felt her heart stop. She'd called her mother a few weeks ago just to let her know where she was, giving her Cal's number to call in case of emergency. Frugal as her mother was, she'd never place a call to Australia unless something was seriously wrong.

Gemma quickly slid off the horse, stumbling as she hit the ground. She landed hard on her backside, crying out in surprise. Cal reached down and pulled her to her feet, then brushed the dirt off her jeans.

"I—I'll be right back," she said.

"I'll come with you," Cal said.

They followed Mary back to the house. She pointed to the phone, lying on the kitchen table but Cal shook his head. "She'll take it in the library," he said.

Gemma hurried through the hall, her heart slamming in her chest. She picked up the phone from the desk. "Mum? Mum, are you there?"

The connection was surprisingly clear. "Gemma.

Good. Finally. I was wondering if you'd ever come on the line. This is costing me a small fortune to call. What kind of hotel is that? Don't you have a phone in your room?"

"What's wrong?" Gemma asked. "Are you all right?"

"Oh, I'm fine, dear. I've had a bit of a cold and my elbow has been sore, but generally, I've been just fine."

"Then why are you calling?"

"Well…I have good news and I have bad. Which would you like first?"

"Mum, this isn't the time for games. You scared me half to death. Why are you calling?"

"Your father needs you," she said, her voice barely containing her excitement.

Gemma shook her head, sure she'd misunderstood. "My father?"

"I had a visit from the Parnell family solicitor yesterday evening and David's asked for you. You have to come home. He wants to see you immediately."

"Why now? After all these years?"

"He's ill, Gemma. He's had some sort of heart attack. He'll be fine, but I suppose it's caused him to think about all the mistakes he's made in the past. It seems he wants to atone for some of them."

"He should be doing that for you, Mum, not me," Gemma snapped. "You're the one who struggled to get by on nothing."

"Gemma, you need to go to him. He's your father. You need to come home right now." She paused. "Before it's too late."

"What does that mean, Mum? He's not going to die. You just said so."

"Before he changes his mind."

"About me? Let him. I don't care. I've wasted too much of my time hoping he'd finally decide to be a father to me. But I'm an adult now. It's time for me to start acting like one."

"You deserve your share of the family trust," her mother said.

"I don't want his money. It's never been about that." She closed her eyes. There had been a time when she would have rushed to David Parnell's side, thrilled that she'd been summoned and eager to do as he demanded.

But why should she give him the satisfaction now? Her father was facing his mortality, so he needed to clear his conscience by making amends for his monstrous behavior. The problem was, she didn't need his approval anymore. She'd found a man who cared about her, who respected her for exactly who she was.

"Please, Gemma. Do this for me. This is what I've been waiting for all these years. I don't think you realize how happy this would make me."

"All right," Gemma murmured. "But I'm not coming home right away. If he's not on his death bed, then he can wait a few days. Bye, Mum." Gemma hung up the phone, then buried her face in her hands. "Oh, God."

"What is it?" Cal asked.

"My father. He's ill and he wants to see me."

Cal was silent for a long time. "That's good," he finally said. "That's what you've wanted all along, right?"

"Yes," Gemma said. "No. I don't know what I want anymore." She looked at him to find concern etched across his handsome features. "I thought this is what I wanted, but now, I'd rather stay here a bit longer."

"Gemma, you have to go. He's your father."

"He's not doing this for me," she said. "He's just being selfish."

"If you don't go, you'll probably regret it. Look at Hayley. She and her grandfather had been at odds for years but she managed to work things out in the end."

"I don't even know my father, beyond a photo my mother kept and a few bits she'd clipped from the newspapers. I've met him twice in my life and both times, he couldn't wait for me to leave. Why should I give him anything he wants?"

"You shouldn't," Cal said. "I don't want you to leave. Let him die with his treatment of you on his conscience. What difference does it make?"

Gemma knew exactly what he was doing, bringing out her better intentions, knowing that in the end, she wouldn't refuse. She leaned in and kissed him, her lips communicating the trust that she'd found in him. "I'll go tomorrow."

"It's the right thing, Gemma. You'll see. And it's not like you're leaving forever."

"It isn't?" Gemma drew back and looked into his eyes. Was this some sort of proposal?

"The station will always be here. And I'll always be on the station. You can come back and visit anytime you like. Take another holiday. You're always welcome."

It was such a simple invitation, Gemma mused. The

kind of thing one would say to any houseguest. Come visit soon. You're welcome anytime. "All right," she said. "As long as you're not married. Who knows, you might find a wife next month. She wouldn't want your old lover showing up at her front door."

It was all so pleasant, this talk of her leaving. Yet inside, every word was like a stab to her heart. She didn't want to hear how easy it would be for Cal to forget her. She wanted him to get down on his knees and beg her to stay, to tell her that he couldn't live without her.

"I don't think that's going to happen," Cal said.

Gemma wanted to press him. What would he do after she left? Would he immediately resume his matrimonial search or would he pine for the Irish girl who'd shared his bed? She wrapped her arms more tightly around his neck and nuzzled her face into a spot beneath his ear.

"I think we should take a nap," she said.

Cal chuckled. "A nap? It's ten in the morning. We just got up a few hours ago."

"I need you lying next to me. With all your clothes off."

"I see. All right. Let's take a nap." He slipped his arms beneath her and stood, carrying her to the door. "I am glad we decided to stay here on the station. A nap is just the kind of adventure one should take on holiday, don't you think?"

CAL STRETCHED OUT ALONG the length of Gemma's naked body, his arm thrown over her waist, his face resting in the curve of her shoulder. He couldn't believe that by this time tomorrow, she would be gone.

It had been nearly a month, yet it seemed like just yesterday when he'd first seen her on the road trying to change her flat tire. He'd sensed that something was about to change in his life at that moment and he'd been right. He'd fallen in love—for the first time.

But would it be the last time? Would his memories of Gemma prevent him from ever inviting another woman into his life? There were so many emotions roiling inside of him. He was angry she'd been manipulated into returning to Ireland by a father she never knew. He was sad he had no choice but to let her go. And he was resigned to the fact that perhaps this was all the time they were meant to have—not even a month. But he'd shown none of these emotions to Gemma.

Callum had decided that their parting would be quiet and easy, exactly the way their relationship had been. There'd be no tears and no last-minute pleas. He'd let her walk away without a fight.

Though he'd extended an invitation for her to return to Kerry Creek, Cal knew the chances of that were slim. She'd slip back into her life in Dublin and thoughts of him would fade. Before long, he'd be just another holiday story, a man she'd met but couldn't quite remember. He pressed a kiss to her neck and sighed.

"Are you awake?" she asked.

"Umm." He kissed her again and pulled her body more tightly against his. "I can't sleep."

She turned toward him, her fingers smoothing over his face. "Neither can I."

"I want to spend every last minute with you. I can sleep in the plane on the way home."

Home. The word cut him like a knife. Her home wasn't here with him. It was in a place he'd never seen, in a country he'd never visited with people he'd never met. He felt as if he understood Gemma better than anyone, yet he knew nothing about her. "Tell me about your life," he said. "You know about mine."

"It's rather ordinary," Gemma said. "I live in a flat near the university. It's small and filled with old books that I inherited from my grandfather. My mother lives not far away, in her own flat, where I go every Monday and Thursday for dinner. When I have time off from my job, I often go to County Clare, to a small cottage that my grandparents left us. It's so pretty, set above the sea on a beautiful green hillside."

"It must be so different from life here on the station."

"It is. It's not dusty. And there are very few blowies or mozzies. It does rain much more, especially in County Clare."

"What about friends? Do you have a lot of friends?"

Gemma shook her head. "Not close friends. I never found much use for that. It's always been difficult for me to trust people." She paused. "You're my friend."

"Really?"

"I trust you, Cal. Completely. I'm not sure why. Maybe it was because of the unfamiliar surroundings. Or maybe getting away from Dublin changed my perspective."

"Besides my brothers, I really don't have any friends, either," he said. "The stockmen are my employees. Mary is like a mother to me. But I understand how you feel. There's no one that I can talk to, the way I can talk to you. I can say anything to you."

"When we first met, I thought you didn't like me. You barely said a word. I thought you could hardly wait until I left Kerry Creek."

"No. I just didn't know how to talk to you. I was nervous. I thought you were the most beautiful woman I'd ever seen in my life and I knew I'd make a fool of myself in front of you. So I just kept my mouth shut until I had something useful to say."

"Until I kissed you. Then you had plenty to say."

"Yeah, that opened the door. I reckoned if you liked me enough to kiss me, you probably would be interested in talking to me, as well."

Gemma giggled as she braced her arms over his chest and stared into his eyes. "We have had a wonderful time."

"Yes, we have," he said.

"And how will you remember it? How will you remember me?"

Cal thought about his response for a long moment. "You're like pure sunshine, all warmth and light, shining on my life for a short time. The sunshine will still be there after you leave, but it will be faded, like it's coming through a curtain."

She pushed up and kissed him, a kiss so sweet it made his heart ache. "That was beautiful."

"It was just the truth, that's all." He reached for her and drew her into another kiss, this one longer and deeper, designed to prove to them both that they couldn't live without each other.

Cal wanted to ask her to stay, to choose between her father and him, her life and his, her future and theirs.

But he knew what it was like for a woman on Kerry Creek. He'd see his mother grow more unhappy with each passing day. And he didn't want that for Gemma. If she were to come back, it would have to be her own decision, without any urging from him.

He rolled her beneath him and settled himself between her legs, slowly moving against her. He'd thought that the sex would be the most difficult thing to give up. But as they teased at each other's bodies with hands and mouths, Cal knew it was just a small part of what they'd shared.

Given the choice, he'd be happy just to have her living in the same house, the same territory, hell, even the same continent, even if it meant giving up sex for the rest of his life. It was her heart and soul he wanted to possess, not just her body.

They continued their conversation as Cal began a slow seduction, afraid that they might not have enough time to say everything that needed saying. But gradually the words turned to sighs and moans and when Cal slipped inside her, he heard her softly whisper his name.

They'd made love enough to know exactly what would please. He slowly brought her close to release, then drew her back, again and again, until Cal wasn't sure he could wait any longer. And when she tumbled over the edge unexpectedly, he let go, joining her in a perfect mingling of their pleasure.

There would never be another woman who could bring him such ecstasy. His heart, his soul and his body would always belong to Gemma, no matter where she was. And though she was walking out of his life in a few hours, Cal had to believe she'd return.

Hope was a funny thing. It could sustain a person in the most difficult of times. It could also blind a person to the realities of life. But for now, hope was all he had.

9

"THANK YOU FOR COMING, GEMMA. I know it meant a lot to him."

Gemma took her stepmother's outstretched hand and shook it, then turned and walked to the front door. A servant stood by, waiting to let her out. When the door closed behind her, Gemma let out a long sigh.

The past hour of her life had been the most bizarre experience she'd ever had. She'd arrived in Belfast a day after landing in Dublin, prepared to face her father for only the third time in her life. But this time, she had the upper hand. She didn't want anything to do with him and yet, he insisted on speaking with her.

Gemma glanced down at the packet of papers clutched in her hand. He'd drawn up documents giving her a share of the Parnell family trust. It was more money than she'd make in twenty years at the university. But unlike her college tuition, it came with no strings attached. He wanted to see her occasionally. And he wanted to know his grandchildren if there ever were any. But she was under no requirement to fulfill his wishes.

Overall, the conversation had been painfully stilted,

with long uncomfortable silences in between. It was far too late for them to enjoy anything resembling a normal relationship. And Gemma wasn't interested in trying.

"Back to the train, miss?"

Gemma smiled at the driver and nodded. "Thank you."

He held the door open and she slipped inside the car, then stared out the window at the huge manor house. With all its beautiful furnishings and expensive art, she preferred the cozy warmth of the homestead on Kerry Creek Station. That was a real home, not a museum filled with remnants of dead ancestors.

She'd left Kerry Creek nearly two days ago. A five-hour drive to Brisbane, a flight to Sydney, a stop in Singapore, a connection in London and then home to Dublin. She hadn't remembered the trip being so long and exhausting on her way to Australia.

But then, she'd been moving toward something. By coming back, she was leaving something—someone— behind. Her thoughts returned to her last moments with Cal, to the kiss he'd given her before helping her into her rental car. Gemma had waited for him to ask her to stay, anxious for the moment when he'd admit he loved her and couldn't live without her.

It hadn't come. He'd simply closed the car door and watched as she drove off. For the first two hours, she'd stop every so often at the side of the road, tempted to turn around and go back, to force him into admitting his feelings.

But then her common sense would return and she'd drive for a bit longer. With every mile that passed, it became more difficult to convince herself she was doing the right thing. Though she might love him, she couldn't make him love her.

Now, tears pressed at the corners of her eyes and she rested her head against the car window, her eyes fixed on the green countryside as it passed by. Where was her home? It certainly wasn't the Parnell country house. And her flat in Dublin didn't feel right, either. Every ounce of her longed for the rugged beauty of outback Queensland.

For a month, Kerry Creek had been her home. But it was more than just the house and land. It was the people. She'd fit in there, like a member of the family. Mary had become a second mother to her and the jackaroos like little brothers. Payton and Hayley were the sisters she'd never had.

Gemma brushed a tear from her cheek. She'd go back someday. Maybe the next summer—or winter, as it was in Australia. But would he be waiting? Or would Cal have moved on, finding a woman who was willing to be a part of his life? She took a ragged breath. Station life wasn't that bad, not when he was there to brighten her days and fill her nights with passion.

But living with him would mean a lot of sacrifices, some she'd never considered ever making for a man. Every shred of common sense told her she was exactly where she was supposed to be. So why couldn't she just accept life as it was?

If Cal had loved her, he would have told her. If he'd wanted her to stay, he would have asked. Gemma drew a deep breath and let it out slowly. Her life here in Ireland was lovely. Until she'd met Cal, it was all she'd ever dreamed it could be.

On the positive side, now she could focus on her work. She'd already decided to write a book about the Irish in Australia. There was a vibrant Irish culture alive in many parts of the country. And after learning more about Crevan and his day-to-day life, she thought she might even attempt a novel, a family saga that would begin on a prison ship and end with a present-day romance.

Gemma smiled. Writing a novel about the Quinns might be just the thing to take her mind off her troubles. She could write a better ending for herself, one where all the obstacles would disappear and she and Cal would live happily ever after. Fiction was a wonderful thing.

"Miss, are you all right?"

Gemma glanced up to see the driver watching her in the rearview mirror. "Me?" She touched her cheeks, surprised to find them wet with tears. "Yes, I'm fine. Just happy, that's all."

"Good," the driver said. "You'll be quite early for the train. Would you like to stop and do some shopping? Or maybe get a bite to eat?"

Gemma shook her head. She needed to get back to familiar surroundings. For now, it would have to be Dublin. But after a week or two with her mother, she was free to do as she pleased. And if she still felt the same way about Cal, maybe a trip back to Kerry Creek wasn't a silly idea.

She'd listen to her heart first and her common sense second. And be open to all the possibilities that the future might hold.

CAL STARED OUT AT THE HORIZON, turning his horse toward the homestead. He was hungry and dirty and he smelled pretty bad. It was time for a hot shower, a decent meal and a good long sleep in his own bed.

After Gemma had left, he'd spent just one night at home, a sleepless night wandering the station, pacing his bedroom, memories of her flooding his brain. So he'd gathered his things and ridden out just after breakfast, needing a place to think. Strangely, he ended up at the creek, at the small camp that he and Gemma had shared. For a moment, he'd regretted taking her there, upset that a visit to the spot would always bring memories of her.

But over the past two days, Cal had come to terms with what he'd had and what he'd lost. It was better to have loved and lost than never to have loved at all. Yes, it was a cliché, but he saw the truth in it. And that truth would have to get him through the next few weeks, months and years without her.

In the distance, Cal could see a pair of horses, with riders perched on them both. He came closer, expecting to find two of the stockmen from the station. But instead, he found his brothers deep in conversation. Cal pulled Eddie to a stop and looked at them both. "Are you having a party without me?"

Brody chuckled. "Where have you been?"

"I took a few days off. I needed some time to myself. When did you get back?"

"About an hour after you rode out. I was going to follow you, but then Mary told me Gemma had left, so I figured you'd want to be alone."

"I wouldn't have been great company. And I'd

reckon you haven't been a joy to live with, either, what with Payton leaving."

"You'd reckon wrong," Teague said, grinning. "Payton came back. I flew her in this morning. She wanted to surprise Brody."

Cal forced a smile. He ought to be happy for his youngest brother and he was. But the feeling was tinged with some bitterness. How wonderful would it have been to return and find that Gemma was the one Teague had brought back? "Where is she?"

"At the homestead," Brody said.

Teague pushed his hat back on his head and braced his hands on his saddle horn. "I'm glad you're back, Cal," he said. "Now that I'm running Wallaroo, I wanted to propose a deal."

"Like the one where I give up the best water bore in Queensland? Like that deal?"

"Well, I'm giving that land back. It's always been Quinn land and it's going to stay that way. Besides, it didn't quite do the trick."

Harry's death had been a shock to everyone. Cal had assumed the old man would outlive them all, just to spite the Quinns. But he'd passed shortly after surgery and had left Wallaroo to both Teague and Hayley. The arrangement hadn't been to Hayley's liking and she'd left Wallaroo the same day Gemma had left Kerry Creek.

"I'm sorry about that," Cal said. "We had our differences, but Harry was still a neighbor. How is Hayley? Have you heard from her?"

Teague shook his head. "No. I don't expect to. She was pretty angry when she left. According to the will, she has to come back within six months, so she'll have some time to cool down."

"So, you have big plans for the place?" Cal asked.

"We're going to raise horses. A small mob to start with. And we have some runs that might be good for Kerry Creek stock."

Cal blinked. First he got his land back and now an offer of grazing land. "What part of Wallaroo are you thinking about?"

Teague pointed to the northeast. "The section that runs up along the tract you gave me. We'd have to add another gate, but we could drive the cattle there after mustering and see how it works out."

"It's good land," Cal said, staring out to the horizon. "And if we have more grazing, we can increase the size of the mob. How many hectares would you want to lease?"

"As much as you want," Teague said.

They discussed terms as Teague explained his plans for the horse-breeding operation. But once again, his brother had a come up with a scheme—this one requiring that Cal give him the Kerry Creek breeding stock in return for Wallaroo grazing rights.

The horse operation had always been Teague's anyway. And it had been much more expensive than raising cattle. Really, Cal was getting the better end of the deal. Land was what he needed in order to expand the Kerry Creek operations. And land was hard to come by, while horses could be purchased almost anywhere.

"He won't go for it," Brody said to Teague. "Cal would never pay for anything that he could get for free."

"That's where you're wrong, little brother." Cal

nodded at Teague. "All right. It's a deal. I'll trade you the Kerry Creek horses for lease rights on Wallaroo."

They chatted about recent events and the women who had come and gone and in Brody's case, had come back again. Cal envied his brothers. They had choices. Both Teague and Brody had the luxury of going anywhere their women were. In fact, Brody and Payton were planning to travel to the States for Brody's tryout with an American football team. And Hayley was only a plane ride away in Sydney. But Gemma was oceans away.

"Maybe you ought to try and convince Gemma to come back," Teague suggested. "Go to Ireland. Explain to her how you feel and ask her to come home with you."

"She wouldn't want to live here," Cal said, shaking his head.

"Why not? If she loves you, she probably won't care where you live," Teague insisted. "And Brody and I can watch over the station while you're gone."

"No, I don't think so."

"What did she say when you asked her to stay?" Brody wondered.

"I didn't ask," Cal replied. "She had to go home. She didn't have a choice. Besides, I didn't want to deal with the rejection."

This started a full-on assault on Cal's stupidity when it came to women, with both Brody and Teague tossing out advice. When he'd had enough of his brothers' haranguing, he pushed his hat down on his head. "I have an idea. Follow me."

With a whoop he kicked Eddie in the flanks and the gelding raced toward the big rock. Teague and Brody followed and when they reached the spot, they climbed to the top and surveyed the land around them.

"Doesn't seem as big as it used to be, does it?" Brody commented.

Brody was right, Cal mused. They used to struggle to climb to the top and now it was quick work.

"So what do we do?" Teague asked. "I'm not sure I remember."

"We have to say it out loud," Cal replied. "One wish. The thing you want most in the world."

"How do we know it will work?" Teague asked.

"It worked for me. Remember?" Brody asked. "I wished I could be a pro footballer. And it happened."

"And I wished I could run a station like Kerry Creek," Cal said. "And I'm running Kerry Creek. I remember what you wished for. You wanted a plane."

"Or a helicopter," Brody said. "I guess you got your wish, too."

"So what makes you think it will work again?" Teague asked.

"We won't know unless we try." Cal drew a deep breath. "I wish Gemma would come back to Kerry Creek for good."

"I wish Hayley would realize I'm the only guy she will ever love."

"I wish Payton would say yes when I ask her to marry me."

Teague and Cal both stared at their little brother, stunned. Brody grinned. "You don't get anything in life unless you ask."

"Well, I guess that's it," Cal said. "We'll see if it

works. Are you riding back to Kerry Creek with us?" he asked Teague.

"I've got work to do at Wallaroo," he said. "But I'll come by tomorrow to talk about our deal."

They jumped off the rock and remounted their horses. Then Brody and Cal headed toward Kerry Creek and Teague toward Wallaroo. As they neared the station, they slowed their pace.

"You should go to her," Brody said. "Plead your case. Show her how you feel."

"No," Cal said. "I can't go to Ireland. Not now. We're going to start mustering tomorrow."

"Put it off," Brody said. "What difference will a week make, Cal? This is the rest of your life we're talking about. You're going to give that up, give up on the woman you love, just because you think it might inconvenience a few cows?"

Cal laughed. "What would I say?"

"Tell her how you feel. It's simple. It's honest. She can't fault you for that."

"Ireland?" Cal said.

"We're not talking about the moon. They do have planes that fly from Oz to Ireland. Do you know where she lives?"

"Not really. We didn't exchange addresses or phone numbers. She knows where to find me. But she did say she taught at the university in Dublin. I suppose I could go there looking for her."

"You could," Brody said.

"But I'd need a ticket. And a passport. I don't have one of those."

"You can get one in Brisbane in a day, maybe two. I don't think you'd need a visa, but we'll have to check on that, too."

Cal thought about the possibilities for a moment or two, then realized it wasn't good to think. Thinking was for fools. Action was what would win him the woman he loved. After all, what did he have to lose? If she said no, then he'd go on with his life as he'd planned. But if she said yes, then everything would change. And like Brody said, he'd never get anything in life unless he asked for it.

"All right," Cal said. "Let's figure out how this is going to happen."

CAL LOOKED UP AT THE OLD buildings of University College. This was Ireland. It was difficult to believe he'd come all this way on a whim. But now that he was here, he realized he was in the land of his ancestors. Somewhere nearby, Crevan had plied his trade as a pickpocket. And somewhere else, he'd been tried, convicted and sentenced to a life in exile.

All around him, the people spoke with a lilt that had come to be familiar to him. But was that because of Gemma or were there still some memories deep in his brain that had been passed along in his DNA? Strangely enough, he felt at home here, as if he belonged.

Cal glanced down at the map he'd purchased at the airport. There'd been some confusion on his arrival whether he'd find her at the University of Dublin or at Trinity College or at University College of Dublin which wasn't in Dublin at all. But a helpful aide at the tourist office found Gemma's name on the staff directory at University College, which was located in an area in southeast Dublin called Belfield.

He walked through the doors of the Newman Building and found the directory, searching for Gemma's name. He'd go first to her office. If he couldn't find her there, then he'd see if they'd give out her phone number. As he walked through the halls of the university, he tried to imagine Gemma working in such an atmosphere. He'd only known her at the station, where she'd set herself up in his messy library, wading through piles of books and stacks of papers.

"May I help you?"

He turned to see an older woman sitting at a desk. Cal smiled. "Do I look lost?"

She nodded. "Who have you come to see?"

"Gemma Moynihan?"

"Her office is just down the corridor and to the left. Her name is on the door. But I don't think she's in. I saw her walking over to the archives about fifteen minutes ago."

"How would I get there?"

"They're in the library. I'll call Seamus and let him know you're coming. What's your name?"

"Quinn," he said. "Callum Quinn."

"You're Australian? And with a name like Quinn, I'd say a bit Irish, too. Here for a visit?"

"Sort of," Cal said. "Which way are the archives?"

"Out through the courtyard and over to James Joyce Library. Once you're there, Seamus will help you. Enjoy your visit, Mr. Quinn."

Cal walked back outside. It seemed as though finding Gemma in Dublin was even more complicated than just getting to Ireland. There were so many places to get lost in a big city.

Cal asked directions along the way and finally found the right building, then was directed through a long series of doors and hallways until he found the archives. A student sat at the desk and watched him suspiciously as he approached. "I'm looking for Gemma Moynihan," Cal said.

"Are you a student?"

"No, a visitor. The lady over in the history building said Seamus would help me locate Gemma."

"She's inside. But you can't go in with that bag," he said, pointing to Cal's duffel. "You'll have to leave that here. Along with some identification." He gave the fellow his passport and set the bag on the floor next to his desk. "Through that door, turn left, go all the way to the end and you'll find some reading tables. I think she's back there."

The archives looked just like the library at Kerry Creek, filled with old books and boxes of papers, only a hundred times larger. He followed the directions, his footsteps echoing softly on the floor. When he turned the corner, Cal stopped.

Gemma was there, bent over a huge book, her hair tumbling down around her face, the light from a reading lamp turning it to spun copper. She reached up and tucked a strand behind her ear and he held his breath as her profile was revealed.

She didn't look different, but in these surroundings, he felt as though he didn't know her at all. He didn't recognize the clothes she wore and she'd painted her fingernails a shocking shade of pink. Had he been a fool to come so far? Drawing a deep breath, Callum took a step forward. "I would have brought tea and bickies, but I didn't have room in my bag."

Gemma jumped at the sound of his voice and turned to him with a stunned expression. Slowly, she pushed her chair back and stood, watching him the whole time as if she wasn't quite sure he was real.

"You have to say something," Cal murmured. "Please tell me I haven't made a mistake in coming."

"Oh, my God," Gemma cried. She crossed the space between them in a heartbeat and threw her arms around his neck. "What are you doing here? How did you find me?"

"It wasn't easy."

"Why are you here? Are you here to see me?"

"You're the only person I know in Dublin, so that would make sense."

"But I've barely been home a week." She pressed a frantic kiss to his lips, then drew back. "Is everything all right?"

"It is now," Cal said. "It's just about perfect."

Gemma ran her hands over his chest. He couldn't believe how much he'd missed her touch. And the effect it had on him. He covered her fingers with his. "You look beautiful," he murmured.

"So do you. Only you seem different. Out of your element." She giggled as she reached up and touched his face. "You got a haircut. And you're wearing the shirt I bought you."

"I wanted to look good."

"It's odd that you would come now," Gemma said,

turning to point to the books scattered on the table. "I've been working on finding the emerald. I think I might have missed something."

"I don't care about the emerald," Callum said.

She grabbed a paper and held it out to him. "See, I found this drawing of the emerald. It's carved with a very specific design. Crevan had probably seen this drawing in court. But this isn't exactly the same design on the emerald in the portrait." She picked up another paper. "This is what's on the portrait. I drew this. And I think Crevan drew his own, from memory, and gave it to the painter." She pulled another paper from the stack. "And then there's this—a drawing of a stone given to the British Royal Family in 1906 by a merchant named Patrick Healy. Recognize it?"

Callum nodded, his gaze shifting back and forth between the two pictures. "So you're saying the royal family has the emerald?"

"I think so," Gemma said. "It looks like Crevan didn't steal it. And I was probably right about him putting it in the portrait as a joke."

Callum smoothed his fingers over her mouth. "A joke that brought you to me. Thank God, Crevan had a sense of humor."

"Don't you understand? If I'd have found this earlier, I never would have come to Australia looking for you. I decided to do an Internet search with a description of the emerald and this came up. So it was more my incompetence than Crevan's joke that took me to Kerry Creek."

"Gemma, I don't care what brought you to me. That's history. This is now."

She nodded, turning into his touch. "Have you come for a visit, then? How long are you staying?"

"Long enough to try to convince you to come back with me," he said. "I know it's a long shot at best, but I have to try. I love you, Gemma. I wasn't sure I'd ever be able to say that to a woman. And I know, if you don't want me, there's never going to be another woman for me. I can live with that."

She opened her mouth to speak and Cal pressed his finger to her lips. "Let me say it all and then you can comment."

Wide-eyed, she nodded her agreement.

"I know the station isn't the most glamorous place to live or the most comfortable. But it's where I have to be, at least for now. But I promise you, we won't be stuck there. We can make a trip to Ireland a couple times a year and stay in your cottage by the sea. And if you want, your mother can come and live with us. There are universities in Brisbane. If you still want to teach, we'll work something out. But we can't live so far apart." Cal paused and drew a deep breath, scanning her face for a clue to her feelings.

"Is that it?" she asked.

He chuckled. "That's it. Oh, and remember, I love you."

She smiled, then ran her hands through the hair at his nape. "I love you, too, Cal."

He waited for the rest. But as seconds ticked by, he got the uneasy feeling that it wouldn't come. Tears swam in her eyes and he watched as one escaped, trickling down her cheek. She wasn't coming home with him. Hell, he'd done what he'd come to do. "I understand, Gemma."

"I don't think you do. I never thought I'd find someone I wanted to spend my life with. And never in a million years did I think that person would live on a cattle station in the Australian outback. But that's where you live. And that's where I'll live if it means I can be with you."

Her words stole the breath from his lungs. Cal gasped, then picked her up off her feet and hugged her hard. "Are you serious? You're not making a galah of me, are you?"

"I don't know what that is," Gemma said. "But I know I'm perfectly serious. I will hold you to your promise about coming back to Ireland, though."

He cupped her face in his hands and kissed her, her mouth soft and warm, the taste like the sweetest wine. "Maybe you should take me to meet your mother," he said. "And then we could pay a visit to that cottage. And while I'm here, I'd like to see where my ancestors came from. Oh, and the Book of Kells." He paused. "I've been reading the tourist brochures."

"We can do all of that. But first I'm taking you home to my flat. You look exhausted."

"I do?"

"Yes, utterly. I think you need a nap."

Cal grinned. "Yes, I do. That's exactly what I need."

She grabbed his hand and they walked toward the door. But Cal had already gone far too long without a kiss. He wrapped his hands around her waist and pressed her back against the shelves, taking possession of her mouth once again.

Of the three Quinn brothers, he'd thought his odds of finding love were the longest. And maybe they had been. But from the moment he'd met Gemma, Cal had known she was meant for him. They'd found each other in a big, wide world full of millions of people. And now that they were together, he intended to make sure her life was happier than she'd ever dreamed.

Epilogue

"It's not that high," Hayley said. "Come on, then, grab my hand. I'll pull you up."

Gemma braced her hands on her waist and looked around. "Don't you find this a wee bit odd? This big rock in the middle of a flat plain. Cal brought me out here one night. It didn't look this big in the dark."

"Teague and I used to meet here all the time when we were kids. He told me it's magic. You stand on top and make a wish and your wish will come true."

Payton took Hayley's hand and scrambled to the top. "Come on, Gemma, it's not that bad."

Gemma grabbed their hands and they hoisted her up to stand next to them. She wobbled a bit, then sat down. It wasn't that hard, she thought to herself. Gemma tipped her face up to the midafternoon sun and closed her eyes, trying to imagine the Quinn brothers as kids. They probably weren't much different than they were now, just a bit smaller.

"I kissed Teague for the first time right here, on this rock," Hayley said, sitting down beside her. "I remember how surprised he was. He'd never kissed a girl before."

"Don't you think it strange that we all ended up here at the same time?" Payton asked, sitting on the other side of Gemma. "What are the chances of that? And now we're all back here, together. At least for a little while."

"Are you leaving?" Gemma asked.

"We're going to the States for Brody's tryout. And then we're going to visit my parents. After that, I'm not sure what we'll be doing…besides getting married."

"Really?" Hayley asked.

Payton nodded. "Who would have thought Brody Quinn was such a traditional guy? He wants the whole nine yards. I'd be happy with a little wedding chapel in Vegas, but that's not enough for Brody."

"Nine yards?" Hayley asked.

"The big wedding, the white dress, the huge cake. But I'm going to try to talk him into something more intimate. Maybe just our families on the beach in Fremantle."

"That sounds lovely," Gemma said. She looked at Hayley. "What about you? Are you and Teague going to have a go at marriage?"

"I suppose we ought to consider it," Hayley replied. She winced. "Since I am going to have a baby."

Gemma and Payton both gasped. "No!" Gemma said. "How could you have kept that a secret from us?"

"I wanted to wait a bit. It's been a few months, so I guess it's safe to tell. Besides, I didn't want the press to get hold of this. I wanted it to belong to us, for just a little while longer."

Payton threw her arms around Hayley and gave her

a fierce hug. "Oh, you and Teague will make beautiful babies together."

"Teague is over the moon. He can't stop talking about it. And he will not leave me alone. He's bought books and DVDs. I still have to finish out my contract with the show, but he's jumping ahead, looking for maternity hospitals. This baby can't come fast enough for his tastes."

They both turned to Gemma. "And what about you, Miss Moynihan?" Payton said. "Now that you're back on Kerry Creek, does Cal intend to make an honest woman of you?"

"He's asked. And I'm considering my answer. I love him, that much I know. And I intend to spend the rest of my life with him. Still, it would be nice to be courted for a while. In any case, I should soon put the poor man out of his misery."

"Speaking of men, look what's coming at us," Peyton said.

Gemma shaded her eyes and watched as three riders approached. "I hope they brought lunch. I'm famished."

"Help me down," Hayley said. "If Teague finds me on this rock, he's going to scold me. I can't walk to the refrigerator without him asking if it will hurt the baby."

Gemma held on to Hayley's hand as she slid to the ground, then dropped down beside her. Payton stayed on top of the rock, smiling as the boys pulled their horses to a stop. "I thought you three were working hard," she said. "Or was it hardly working?"

Brody wagged his finger at her. "You better crawl down before you fall down."

"Come and get me."

He jumped off his horse and scampered up the rock, then grabbed her around the waist and kissed her. Hayley stood beside Teague, her hand on his thigh, his fingers laced through hers.

Gemma looked up at Cal. Even covered in a layer of dust, he was still the most stunning man she'd ever seen in her life. He smiled at her, the kind of smile she'd seen the night before, after he'd made love to her. It told her everything she needed to know.

"Yes," Gemma said.

"Yes?" he asked.

She nodded. "To that question you've been waiting on. The answer is yes."

Cal jumped off his horse, grabbed her around the waist and kissed her, picking her up off the ground as their mouths met. "Yes," he said, his breath warm against her ear.

Gemma closed her eyes and held tight as he spun her around. For a moment, she was dizzy, but then he kissed her again and everything became clear. This was exactly where she belonged, in his arms, in his life. There was no longer any doubt and there never would be again.

* * * * *

Celebrate Harlequin's 60th anniversary with
Harlequin® Superromance®
and the DIAMOND LEGACY miniseries!

Follow the stories of four cousins as they come to
terms with the complications of love and what it
means to be a family. Discover with them the
sixty-year-old secret that rocks not one but two
families in…
A DAUGHTER'S TRUST by Tara Taylor Quinn.

Available in September 2009 from
Harlequin® Superromance®.

RICK'S APPOINTMENT with his attorney early Wednesday morning went only moderately better than his meeting with social services the day before. The prognosis wasn't great—but at least his attorney was going to file a motion for DNA testing. Just so Rick could petition to see the child…his sister's baby. The sister he didn't know he had until it was too late.

The rest of what his attorney said had been downhill from there.

Cell phone in hand before he'd even reached his Nitro, Rick punched in the speed-dial number he'd programmed the day before.

Maybe foster parent Sue Bookman hadn't received his message. Or had lost his number. Maybe she didn't want to talk to him. At this point he didn't much care what she wanted.

"Hello?" She answered before the first ring was complete. And sounded breathless.

Young and breathless.

"Ms. Bookman?"

"Yes. This is Rick Kraynick, right?"

"Yes, ma'am."

"I recognized your number on caller ID," she said,

her voice uneven, as though she was still engaged in whatever physical activity had her so breathless to begin with. "I'm sorry I didn't get back to you. I've been a little…distracted."

The words came in more disjointed spurts. Was she jogging?

"No problem," he said, when, in fact, he'd spent the better part of the night before watching his phone. And fretting. "Did I get you at a bad time?"

"No worse than usual," she said, adding, "Better than some. So, how can I help?"

God, if only this could be so easy. He'd ask. She'd help. And life could go well. At least for one little person in his family.

It would be a first.

"Mr. Kraynick?"

"Yes. Sorry. I was… Are you sure there isn't a better time to call?"

"I'm bouncing a baby, Mr. Kraynick. It's what I do."

"Is it Carrie?" he asked quickly, his pulse racing.

"How do you know Carrie?" She sounded defensive, which wouldn't do him any good.

"I'm her uncle," he explained, "her mother's— Christy's—older brother, and I know you have her."

"I can neither confirm nor deny your allegations, Mr. Kraynick. Please call social services." She rattled off the number.

"Wait!" he said, unable to hide his urgency. "Please," he said more calmly. "Just hear me out."

"How did you find me?"

"A friend of Christy's."

"I'm sorry I can't help you, Mr. Kraynick," she said softly. "This conversation is over."

"I grew up in foster care," he said, as though that gave him some special privilege. Some insider's edge.

"Then you know you shouldn't be calling me at all."

"Yes… But Carrie is my niece," he said. "I need to see her. To know that she's okay."

"You'll have to go through social services to arrange that."

"I'm sure you know it's not as easy as it sounds. I'm a single man with no real ties and I've no intention of petitioning for custody. They aren't real eager to give me the time of day. I never even knew Carrie's mother. For all intents and purposes, our mother didn't raise either one of us. All I have going for me is half a set of genes. My lawyer's on it, but it could be weeks— months—before this is sorted out. Carrie could be adopted by then. Which would be fine, great for her, but then I'd have lost my chance. I don't want to take her. I won't hurt her. I just have to see her."

"I'm sorry, Mr. Kraynick, but…"

* * * * *

*Find out if Rick Kraynick will ever have a chance
to meet his niece.
Look for A DAUGHTER'S TRUST
by Tara Taylor Quinn,
available in September 2009.*

HARLEQUIN
60 YEARS
of pure reading pleasure

We'll be spotlighting a different series
every month throughout 2009
to celebrate our 60th anniversary.

Look for Harlequin® Superromance®
in September!

THE DIAMOND Legacy

*Celebrate with
The Diamond Legacy
miniseries!*

Follow the stories of four cousins as they come to terms
with the complications of love and what it means to
be a family. Discover with them the sixty-year-old secret
that rocks not one but two families.

A DAUGHTER'S TRUST by *Tara Taylor Quinn*
September

FOR THE LOVE OF FAMILY by *Kathleen O'Brien*
October

LIKE FATHER, LIKE SON by *Karina Bliss*
November

A MOTHER'S SECRET by *Janice Kay Johnson*
December

Available wherever books are sold.

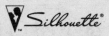

SPECIAL EDITION

FROM *NEW YORK TIMES* BESTSELLING AUTHOR

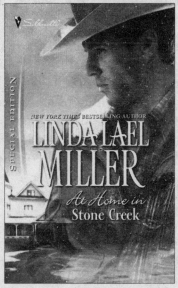

Ashley O'Ballivan had her heart broken by a man years
ago—and now he's mysteriously back. Jack McCall *isn't*
the person she thinks he is. For her sake, he must keep
his distance, but his feelings for her are powerful.
To protect her—from his enemies and himself—he
has to leave...vowing to fight his way home to
her and Stone Creek forever.

Available in November wherever books are sold.

Visit Silhouette Books at www.eHarlequin.com

SSE65487

You're invited to join our Tell Harlequin Reader Panel!

By joining our new reader panel you will:

- Receive Harlequin® books—they are FREE and yours to keep with no obligation to purchase anything!
- Participate in fun online surveys
- Exchange opinions and ideas with women just like you
- Have a say in our new book ideas and help us publish the best in women's fiction

In addition, you will have a chance to win great prizes and receive special gifts!
See Web site for details. Some conditions apply.
Space is limited.

To join, visit us at
www.TellHarlequin.com.

REQUEST YOUR FREE BOOKS!

2 FREE NOVELS PLUS 2 FREE GIFTS!

HARLEQUIN® Blaze™

Red-hot reads!

YES! Please send me 2 FREE Harlequin® Blaze™ novels and my 2 FREE gifts (gifts are worth about $10). After receiving them, if I don't wish to receive any more books, I can return the shipping statement marked "cancel". If I don't cancel, I will receive 6 brand-new novels every month and be billed just $4.24 per book in the U.S. or $4.71 per book in Canada. That's a savings of 15% off the cover price. It's quite a bargain. Shipping and handling is just 50¢ per book.* I understand that accepting the 2 free books and gifts places me under no obligation to buy anything. I can always return a shipment and cancel at any time. Even if I never buy another book, the two free books and gifts are mine to keep forever.

151 HDN EYS2   351 HDN EYTE

Name	(PLEASE PRINT)	
Address		Apt. #
City	State/Prov.	Zip/Postal Code

Signature (if under 18, a parent or guardian must sign)

Mail to the **Harlequin Reader Service:**
IN U.S.A.: P.O. Box 1867, Buffalo, NY 14240-1867
IN CANADA: P.O. Box 609, Fort Erie, Ontario L2A 5X3

Not valid to current subscribers of Harlequin Blaze books.

Want to try two free books from another line?
Call 1-800-873-8635 or visit www.morefreebooks.com.

* Terms and prices subject to change without notice. Prices do not include applicable taxes. N.Y. residents add applicable sales tax. Canadian residents will be charged applicable provincial taxes and GST. Offer not valid in Quebec. This offer is limited to one order per household. All orders subject to approval. Credit or debit balances in a customer's account(s) may be offset by any other outstanding balance owed by or to the customer. Please allow 4 to 6 weeks for delivery. Offer available while quantities last.

Your Privacy: Harlequin Books is committed to protecting your privacy. Our Privacy Policy is available online at www.eHarlequin.com or upon request from the Reader Service. From time to time we make our lists of customers available to reputable third parties who may have a product or service of interest to you. If you would prefer we not share your name and address, please check here.

HB09R3

HARLEQUIN® Blaze™

COMING NEXT MONTH
Available August 25, 2009

#489 GETTING PHYSICAL Jade Lee
For American student/waitress Zoe Lewis, Tantric sex—sex as a spiritual experience—is a totally foreign concept. Strange, yet irresistible. Then she's partnered with Tantric master Stephen Chiu…and discovers just how far great sex can take a girl!

#490 MADE YOU LOOK Jamie Sobrato
Forbidden Fantasies
She spies with her little eye… From the privacy of her living room Arianna Day has a front-row seat for her neighbor Noah Quinn's sex forays. And she knows he's the perfect man to end her bout of celibacy. Now to come up with the right plan to make him look…

#491 TEXAS HEAT Debbi Rawlins
Encounters
Four college girlfriends arrive at the Sugarloaf ranch to celebrate an engagement announcement. With all the tasty cowboys around, each will have a reunion weekend she'll never forget!

#492 FEELS LIKE THE FIRST TIME Tawny Weber
Dressed to Thrill
Zoe Gaston hated high school. So the thought of going back for her reunion doesn't exactly thrill her. Little does she guess that there's a really hot guy who's been waiting ten long years to do just that!

#493 HER LAST LINE OF DEFENSE Marie Donovan
Uniformly Hot!
Instructing a debutante in survival training is not how Green Beret Luc Boudreau planned to spend his temporary leave. Problem is, he kind of likes this feisty fish out of water and it turns out the feeling's mutual. But will they find any common ground other than their shared bedroll…?

#494 ONE GOOD MAN Alison Kent
American Heroes: The Texas Rangers
Jamie Danby needs a hero—badly. As the only witness to a brutal shooting, she's been flying below the radar for years. Now her cover's blown and she needs a sexy Texas Ranger around 24/7 to make her feel safe. The best sex of her life is just a bonus!

www.eHarlequin.com